"Tell me insisted

He leaned forward on his elbows and his voice grew softer, deeper. "I want to hear all about your fantasies. Tell me, Zara. Tell me everything."

Emma bit her lip. Zara. It was Zara he wanted. Zara he desired. Of course. Emma was only temporarily wearing Zara's clothes, not to mention her man-killer rep. Of course he wanted Zara. Everyone wanted Zara.

He zeroed in on her mouth, and she suddenly saw herself from his perspective—a flushed young woman, dark hair askew, eyes glittering with sexual excitement. Looking just like Zara.

She felt beautiful…desirable. She'd never felt this way before, never felt the heat of a man's gaze, the hunger, the wanting….

She liked it. It thrilled her, and her heart raced with anticipation….

Dear Reader,

When Harlequin asked us to write two books featuring twin heroines, they didn't have to ask twice! As identical twins ourselves, we knew we'd have a blast with this unique project.

Along with the creative challenge came a geographical one: We live four hundred miles apart! However, between occasional road trips and daily phone calls (our twin telepathy was on the fritz), we brainstormed a dynamite story that begins here with *Twice the Spice,* and ends in Pam's May Intrigue title, *Twice Burned.*

We've woven tender romance and sizzling passion into a story rife with mistaken identity, heart-thumping danger, stunning plot twists and more than one dark secret. While each book stands on its own, we urge you to double your pleasure by reading both.

Our twin heroines, Emma and Zara, are close to our hearts. Their special bond gives them the strength and courage to overcome all odds. And as for Gage and Logan...we think you'll fall in love with both of them, just as we did!

We'd love to hear from you. Write to us at Harlequin Enterprises Ltd., 225 Duncan Mill Road, Don Mills, Ontario M3B 3K9, Canada.

Happy reading!

Sincerely,

Patricia Ryan and Pamela Burford

Books by Patricia Ryan

HARLEQUIN TEMPTATION
540—THE RETURN OF THE BLACK SHEEP
571—A BURNING TOUCH
602—FOR THE THRILL OF IT

TWICE THE SPICE
Patricia Ryan

Harlequin Books

TORONTO • NEW YORK • LONDON
AMSTERDAM • PARIS • SYDNEY • HAMBURG
STOCKHOLM • ATHENS • TOKYO • MILAN
MADRID • WARSAW • BUDAPEST • AUCKLAND

For my very own
Evil Twin,
Pamela Burford.
This is another fine
kettle of fish
you've gotten us into.

ISBN 0-373-25731-7

TWICE THE SPICE

Copyright © 1997 by Patricia Ryan.

Printed in U.S.A.

1

"I'M GONNA SELL Mom's ray gun."

"You're gonna sell what?" Hunching her shoulder to bring the portable phone more firmly against her ear, Emma Sutcliffe squatted down to slice open one of the twenty-three boxes piled up in the living room of her new house.

"The ray gun." Zara's voice sounded distant and crackly. No wonder. She was on the other side of the world. "You know. The one she used in *Reptile Bride*."

Emma cracked open the box, on which she'd scrawled "Mysteries, *Q-T*," removed her carefully folded list of its contents and trailed her fingers lovingly over the paperbacks within. "You mean *Atomic Bride*."

Zara sighed. "Whatever."

"Wait a minute." Emma scooped out a double handful of tattered whodunits and rose to slide them into one of the eight bookcases she'd bought at garage sales and refinished. "I think it was *Return of the Atomic Bride*. That was the one with the ray guns. They used flamethrowers in *Atomic Bride*, remember?"

"No," Zara snapped across the thousands of phone-line miles that separated them. "I don't remember. I'm afraid I have better things to do with my life than commit every detail of Candy Carmelle's movie career to memory."

"This is our *mother's* movie career we're talking about

here," Emma said. "But, as usual, you're too wrapped up in being *fabulous* to pay any attention to—"

"Excuse me?" Zara's voice turned shrill. Emma instantly regretted having goaded her. She kept promising herself—they both kept promising each other—that they'd try to keep from combusting on contact. On the one hand, they were closer to each other than to anyone else on earth, having been cut, as it were, from the same yard of cloth. Deep down, they shared a love that nothing would ever touch. But when identical twins turned into polar opposites, with completely different views of the world, just getting along became a monumental challenge. "In case it's escaped your notice, Emma, I've been paying a heck of a *lot* of attention to Mom lately. It's been kind of unavoidable, considering she's been *living* with me for the past month. Her and her ray guns and rubber brains and swamp-monster flippers. I've got walls I paid seven thousand dollars to have sponge-painted a couple of years ago, and she—"

"You paid seven thousand dollars for that? I just wrote an article on sponge-painting for *Family Digest*. You could have done it yourself for about twenty bucks."

Zara dismissed that notion with an incredulous snort. "Can't you just see me in my little painter's overalls and cap?" Somehow Emma couldn't. "I had the walls done P.D. Predivorce. Money was no object then. Anyway, I've got these gorgeous, expensive walls, and Mom went and Scotch-taped movie posters all over them. And that's not all. She changed my answering-machine message. Now when people call me to negotiate million-dollar deals, they hear her screeching, 'They're coming! Don't you see them? You must see them!'"

"That's her big speech from *The Slithering*," Emma offered.

"And then she shrieks in terror until the beep comes. You

can't imagine what it's been like, sharing an apartment with Ye Olde Scream Queen."

Now it was Emma's turn to sigh. "Yes, I can." She'd been imagining it a lot lately—ever since last month, when Candy Carmelle had had a falling-out with her much younger boyfriend and stormed out of his houseboat. Candy had spent the last of her savings on a bus ticket from Florida to Manhattan, showing up at Zara's apartment on Easter Sunday with three trunks full of old movie props and an expectation of permanent residency.

Emma recalled Zara's panicked phone call and the deal they'd struck. As Candy's only children, the twins would take turns providing a home for her, starting, by default, with Zara. Emma's first turn would commence as soon as she'd gotten settled into her new house. If this had happened before Zara's ugly divorce last year, Zara would simply have bought Candy her own place and that would have been that. But she had gotten socked with having to pay Tony a hefty settlement and had been rebuilding her bank account ever since.

"So, are you all moved in yet?" Zara asked hopefully.

"No." Emma grabbed another two fistfuls of books and jammed them in the bookcase, careful to keep the authors in alphabetical order.

"Well, *get* moved in. As soon as I get back from Australia, you're getting Mom."

Emma bit her lip and thought fast. "I really need some time to get the place—"

"Save it, Em."

Emma shook her head at the futility of trying to dicker with a merciless negotiator like Zara Sutcliffe. "When will you be coming back?"

"Dunno. I should have been back already, but the situation here is incendiary, and I can't leave now."

All Emma knew about "the situation here" was what Liz Smith had reported on the news last night:

"Glamorous literary superagent Zara Sutcliffe has been getting more ink than her celebrated clients lately. Not only has she become something of a fixture in the New York and L.A. club scenes, but she's been making headlines with some pretty impressive hardcover-slash-movie deals. Well, trouble is brewing on the set of one of those movies, *Thunder in the Outback*, being filmed on location in Australia. Seems her client, novelist-screenwriter Maxine Moore, has gotten a bee in her bonnet over changes to the script, the upshot of which is that she, the producer, the director and half the cast are all threatening to sue each other. Ms. Sutcliffe was called in to defuse the situation. Ladies and gentlemen, I know some of the parties involved, and if she can pull this one off, it will be nothing short of a miracle."

Zara was talking about the ray gun again, and how she was going to sell it, and how that would solve all their Candy Carmelle problems forever.

"Wait a minute." Emma dumped her handful of books back in the box and held her palm up, like a cop directing traffic. "Back up and start over." Like Zara, Emma loved her mother. She adored her mother, despite her eccentricities; sometimes *because* of them. But no way did she want to live with her mother. Moving from bucolic rural Maine to this dismal little rented house in Queens, New York, had been traumatic enough; throwing Candy Carmelle into the mix would turn a difficult situation into a nightmare. If there was an alternative to that, she wanted to hear it.

"Okay, here's the scoop," Zara said. "A man called the

apartment last Saturday and asked for Mom. She was out getting a facial, so I offered to take a message. I recognized the guy's name—MacGowan Byrne. He deals in hard-to-find collectibles. One of my authors, who's pushing ninety, sold him a complete set of her first editions last year, but of course he robbed her—she should have consulted me first. Anyway, he has this mysterious client who wants to fill out his collection of movie weapons, and he's looking for guess what."

"The ray gun from *Return of the Atomic Bride*."

"Bingo. He wanted me to talk to Mom, 'cause he heard she'd kept lots of props from her movies. I told him she had the ray gun, but he'd have to deal with me."

"Why?"

"*Why?* For one thing, she'd probably refuse to even consider selling off one of her precious props. Even if she were willing to, can you see her negotiating a price? I cut deals for a living. Guess how much he offered for it."

Emma rolled her eyes. "Gee, I dunno, Zara. What's the Blue Book value on ray guns this year?"

"Come on—take a guess."

"It's a *ray gun*, Zara. I can't begin to imagine what someone would be willing to pay for something like that, or why he'd even want it, for that matter."

"He offered three thousand dollars," Zara said.

"Seriously? Holy cow! Someone's gonna pay three thousand dollars for that worthless—"

"Of course not."

"Huh?"

"I got him up to two million," Zara announced smugly. Emma snorted. "Har har."

Another languorous transcontinental sigh floated over the phone lines. "You would have given it away for a measly three thou, wouldn't you? No, don't answer that. It's too scary to contemplate."

Emma squinted at a curtainless window with a torn plastic shade. "Be straight with me, Zara. This is us. How much is he really gonna—"

"Two million big ones, sis. You shouldn't be so surprised. It's kind of insulting, you know. I do this kind of stuff for a living. I'm famous the world over for my cutthroat deals, and here you're suggesting I'd give up a valuable collectible for—"

"Valuable? Collectible? It's a toy gun, for cryin' out loud. A forgotten prop from a 1966 horror movie no one even remembers."

"That's where you're wrong," Zara said with irritating patience, "and that's why it's a good thing *I* was in charge of this deal. That gun is far from forgotten. Someone remembers it very well. And wants it very badly."

"Who? Who in their right mind would be willing to pay that kind of money for a *ray gun?*"

"Mac's very—"

"Mac?"

"MacGowan Byrne," Zara said. "Everyone calls him Mac. He's very secretive—he won't reveal his client's name. Somebody famous, probably, who doesn't want any publicity. As for being in his right mind, you can forget that. Collectors are crazy. If they get fixated on getting something, they'll pay anything for it. Up to a point, of course. In my line of work, you develop a sixth sense for somebody's top price, and in this case, I knew it was two mill."

"Wait a minute. This collector—this anonymous nut job who can't live without that ray gun—authorized Mac to go from three thousand to *two million?*"

"Could be he just offered Mac a chunk of change and

said, 'Get it for me.' That's the way these things work some-times. Of course, once the dealer locates the object, he tries to pay as little as possible for it, 'cause the difference be-tween what he pays and what the collector pays him is his profit.''

"So the collector is paying this Mac guy even *more* than two million?"

"I assume so, otherwise he wouldn't have accepted my price. I don't know and I don't really care, but I'll tell you one thing." Zara chuckled with evident self-satisfaction. "He's making a lot less of a profit than he thought he would. That's the last time he'll underestimate the negoti-ating savvy of Zara Sutcliffe, I can tell you that."

Something in Zara's tone set off Emma's uh-oh alarm. Hiding beneath her sister's brash self-confidence, she knew, was a wobbly kneed little girl trying to prove herself. Ninety-nine percent of the time, Zara Sutcliffe was the shrewd, eerily unflappable businesswoman the press por-trayed her to be. But every once in a while someone would push that button of hers—usually by acting condescending or otherwise underestimating her, on account of her looks or glamorous reputation—and she'd turn back into the de-fensive, I'll-show-everybody child she'd once been. It didn't happen often, but when it did, her knee-jerk re-sponse was to haggle the offending party to his knees, and then some. They'd walk away from the table defeated, per-plexed...and often angry. From the sound of it, this Mac-Gowan Byrne had been on the receiving end of Zara's ne-gotiating wrath, and that made Emma nervous.

"Who is this guy, really?" Emma asked. "What do you know about him, except that he ripped off one of your au-thors for her first editions?"

"I investigated him." Zara sounded almost indignant. "He's legit."

"Define *investigated*."

"I asked around. He's an established dealer in art and collectibles."

"You know, Zara, there's more to investigating someone than 'asking around.' A thorough background check would have revealed his credit record, any criminal history, business improprieties..."

Zara laughed derisively. "And now for another episode of Emma Sutcliffe, Girl P.I."

"Doesn't it make you nervous, knowing so little about this guy?"

"I know enough."

Emma changed tack. "What does Mom know?"

"Mom?"

"Have you told her about this yet?" Emma asked.

There came a pause. "See..."

"Were you planning on telling her?"

"See, this is the thing, Emma."

"Were you?"

"If we go ahead and sell it, then give her the money, it's a done deal. She'll be two million dollars richer. She can invest it in mutual funds, or maybe an annuity, and live comfortably—more than comfortably—for the rest of her life. She can finance that exercise video she keeps talking about. She can travel. But most important, she can buy her own place."

"She'll be mad at us," Emma warned.

"Furious. But she'll get over it. On the other hand, if we ask her permission first, more than likely she'll say no. You know her—she's horrifically sentimental about all that movie junk. And after all, what does she need money for? She has no expenses as long as she's living with us. We're not gonna charge her room and board. We're just gonna put up with her, day after day, year after year, decade after—"

"Oh, boy," Emma moaned, sinking cross-legged to the floor.

"So you'll go along with selling the ray gun?"

Emma hesitated. "I need time to think about it."

"You always 'need time to think about it.' That's the story of your life, Emma."

"I don't like to rush into things."

"Correction—you're terrified of rushing into things. I worry about you, honey. Really. I'm not saying this to be a bitch, believe it or not, I'm saying it because I care. You're terrified of change, of making decisions, of meeting new people, of taking risks.... Don't you ever stop and wonder whether you're missing anything?"

All the time, Emma thought soberly.

"Life is passing you by, Emma."

No kidding.

"I'm amazed you got it together to move."

So am I. Relocating had been the hardest thing she'd ever had to do, but she'd had no choice. When *CraftWorld*, which had published most of her freelance articles, bit the dust, she'd been forced by economic necessity to take the staff job that *Crafty Lady* offered. Only that had meant moving to New York City. Writing articles about "Festive EZ-Quilt Holiday Vests" and "Brightening your Life with Decoupage Switchplates" had long since lost its charm, and now she'd get to do it full-time, and have a boss and a little cubicle, and live in this swarming hellhole of a city to boot. And she'd have even less time to finish plotting that whodunit she'd been meaning to write for about the last ten years. At least she'd been able to afford—barely—to rent this house instead of an apartment; she didn't think she could have borne not having a yard. During the three days since her arrival in Queens, she'd done little but unpack. She hadn't summoned up the courage to take the subway into Manhattan yet and was grateful that she didn't have to report to work for another week.

"What'll it be?" Zara prodded. "I need to know right now whether you'll go along with this, because Mac is gonna be waiting for me with a cashier's check for two million big ones at his office in SoHo this afternoon."

Emma lay on her back and rubbed her eyes. "Has it occurred to you there's just one tiny problem here?"

"I'm stuck in Australia and the deal's going down in New York this afternoon?"

"Why do I suddenly feel the walls closing in?" Emma muttered.

"Under normal circumstances," Zara said, "I'd just have one of my staff handle it, but Mac won't deal with anybody but me. He warned me not to even tell anybody else about the sale, or it'd be off. And I can't postpone the meeting, 'cause there was no answer when I tried to call the phone number he gave me."

Emma swallowed hard. "I don't like where this is heading."

"My picture's been in all the gossip columns lately, so he knows what I look like, and how I dress."

Like a thousand-dollar-a-night call girl, Emma thought.

"So you'll have to stop by my place and change into one of my outfits. Some makeup wouldn't hurt, either. Mom will let you in. And then you'll have to go to my office and get the ray gun. I sneaked it out of the apartment the other day. It's in the credenza next to my desk. Let my staff think you're me—remember, this deal is supposed to be a secret. Tell them you decided to come back early from Australia. Then you can cab down to SoHo." Zara rattled off an address in the artsy lower-Manhattan neighborhood.

Emma sat up, gripping the phone way too hard. "This is crazy, Zara. I can't just agree to something like this on the spur of the moment."

"I tried to call you yesterday, when I realized I wouldn't be back in time, but they told me your new phone number was unlisted. Who do you think you are—Madonna?"

"I don't like strangers having my phone number."

"I called Mom for it, but she wasn't in, so I had to keep trying her—"

"Well, fine, but I'm still gonna need time to—"

"Well, you don't have it!" Zara snapped. "Stop being such a dweeb, Emma! You cannot take a wait-and-see attitude this time. Your choice is simple. Either sell that ray gun or spend the next God-knows-how-many decades sharing living quarters with the Queen of the B's."

"Oh, boy."

"It's what, about two-thirty there? You've got two and a half hours to turn into me, get the ray gun and make it to SoHo. You remember where I live, right? The Sans Souci, on East 86th?"

"I remember," Emma groaned. "Oh, I hate this."

"And my office is on 60th between Third and—"

"I know where it is, but I can't do this."

"Do it, Emma."

"Zara...can't we just talk about—"

"Just do it." *Click.*

"Wait a minute." Emma shook the phone, like an idiot. "Where can I reach you if... *Darn it!*" She hauled back to throw the phone across the room, but then thought better of it. It might break. Or it might hit a window, and then she'd have to call a glazier in, and she hated having strangers in her home. Or it might nick the wall, which wasn't as bad, but she'd still have to fix it, or at least put a bookcase in front of it....

Zara's right, she thought gloomily as she turned the phone off and laid it carefully on the floor. *I'm a total dweeb*.

"HONEY, DO YOU KNOW where my ray gun is?" Candy Carmelle asked Emma as she held open the door to Zara's Upper East Side apartment.

Uh-oh. As her mother closed the door behind her, Emma stepped warily into the foyer, wishing desperately she was the kind of person who could think on her feet.

"What am I saying?" Candy unwrapped a stick of gum and slid it between her frosted-coral lips, then tossed the crumpled wrapper onto a delicate little glass table. "You wouldn't know. You're never here." She frowned at Emma, and even that didn't produce much in the way of wrinkles around her sharp blue eyes. Candy Carmelle's skin was smooth and taut, the product of lucky genes, a lifelong aversion to the sun and, Emma suspected, an occasional bit of surgical intervention. Emma wasn't sure what color her mother's hair really was, since she'd been a bottle blonde of one shade or another for the entire twenty-nine years and eleven months that Emma had been alive. Judging from the roots, she was probably a dark brunette, like her twin daughters.

Emma realized she must have caught her mother in mid-workout. A gleaming unitard hugged her well-honed body like silver spray paint. Even without the cone bras and girdles that had shaped her to Cold-War perfection for the silver screen, Candy Carmelle was *built*. She looked like a cartoon of a blond bombshell. No one meeting her for the first time would ever guess she was sixty-one years old.

Candy's gaze swept her daughter from head to toe, cataloging with obvious distaste Emma's T-shirt and jeans. "Sweetie, I've told you a million times—you'll never have any kind of social life, dressing like that." "Social life" meaning, of course, male attention.

Emma closed her eyes and expelled a lengthy sigh. "Mom—"

"Virginity's not a healthy condition, you know." Candy's tone of gentle, maternal concern was punctuated by a sharp crack of gum. "Not at your age."

Emma took a deep, pacifying breath. "Mom, where's Zara's bedroom? I have to change...I'm gonna borrow some of her clothes."

Candy's eyebrows disappeared into her yellow bangs. "I thought you hated the way she dresses."

"I thought so, too." Rubbing her eyes, Emma concentrated on quelling the latest in the series of panic attacks that had begun when she decided, forty-five minutes ago, that she was actually going to go along with Zara on this lunatic scheme.

"I don't get it, then. How come you want to borrow her clothes? You got a date or something? That's it, isn't it? You actually landed a date, and now you've got nothing to wear."

"That's it," Emma muttered, the lie somewhat mitigated by her mother's having thought it up.

"Come on, then—let's get you fixed up."

Emma followed her through an archway flanked by a pair of faux-marble columns and into Zara's formerly sleek and stylish apartment, noting with a mixture of amusement and apprehension her mother's additions to the decor. Ragged posters with protoplasmic lettering screaming *House of Blood, Dr. Blood* and *Blood Wedding*—"In Bloodcolor!"—adorned the badly sponge-painted seven-thousand-dollar walls; an unnervingly realistic decapitated head, festooned with electrodes, glowered at her from beneath a glass dome on the elegant lacquered coffee table; The Brain from Aster-

oid X floated in a jar of phosphorescent green mystery fluid
in an illuminated nook in the wall.

Everywhere Emma looked there was something to look
away from: plastic body parts in various stages of simu-
lated decay; shrunken mummies' hands; tarantulas; eyeballs; miniature rocket ships; diminutive flying saucers;
tiny robots; howling monster masks; shiny pseudoscientific
gizmoids; various eggs, pods, spores, sprouts and mutated
tubers of every conceivable size and shape.

Scattered among these rather alarming souvenirs was the
detritus of Candy Carmelle's disordered life—newspapers,
magazines, diet-ginger-ale cans, gum wrappers, discarded
clothing, dirty dishes.... No wonder Zara was flipping out.
Like Emma, she was a neat freak, in her own way; it was
the only thing the two of them had in common. That, and
their baffling but deep affection for their one-of-a-kind
mother.

There was another thing about Candy Carmelle that
made her unbearable to live with, Emma realized, even
more than the chaos she generated. Candy's very person-
ality tended to fill up a room. When she was around, there
just wasn't a whole lot of psychic space left over for anyone
else. It dawned on Emma with abrupt clarity that she
would never, *ever* be able to live with her mother. She
wouldn't survive it—not with her sanity intact. This awareness reinforced her sense of purpose; she had to impersonate Zara and pull off the sale of the ray gun. She had to.
Nothing had ever felt more imperative.

Zara's bedroom was an antiseptic refuge in the midst of
all that clutter and confusion: white walls, white bed-
spread, white curtains.... Emma slid out of her loafers and
left them outside the door.

"Her clothes are in there." Candy pointed toward a large
dressing room with built-in closets and drawers and a

three-way mirror, then flopped down on the bed and grabbed the TV remote. Emma checked her watch: 3:20. She'd better hustle.

She whipped through the items hanging in the closets, dismayed to find not a single skirt reaching below mid-thigh. Settling on the least provocative garment—a canary yellow leather suit—she started tugging open drawers, looking for something to wear underneath it.

Looks like Victoria's Secret in here. Drawer after drawer was filled with nothing but push-up demi bras, abbreviated bikini underwear and garter belts, all in matching sets. They were the kinds of things women wore to tempt men, Emma reflected as she idly fingered the seductive little scraps of lace and silk. *Virginity's not a healthy condition,* her mother had said. *Not at your age.*

Life is passing you by, Emma, Zara had said, and she was right. At this rate, Emma would still be in full possession of her increasingly pointless and embarrassing chastity on June 10, which happened to be less than a month away, and also happened to be her thirtieth birthday. Her stomach burned with anxiety at the prospect of turning thirty with her sexual innocence intact. In her mother's day they would have called her a spinster, or maybe an old maid. Nowadays they called women like her neurotic.

Emma cleared her throat. "Where's her panty hose?" she yelled toward the bedroom, where she could hear muffled conversation from the TV—one of those shock talk shows.

Candy's gum popped. "She doesn't have any."

Perfect. Emma grimaced as she kicked off her jeans and pulled her T-shirt over her head. "What blouse does she wear under that yellow leather suit?" she called out.

"She doesn't," Candy replied.

Great. Emma slipped on the short, tight jacket and fastened the snaps that secured it in front, only to find her bra peeking out above the low neckline.

Just fine. Stripping off the jacket, she exchanged her modest white bra for one of Zara's black satin push-up numbers, then resnapped the jacket. It fit like it had been sewn on, and Emma was startled to note a subtle hint of cleavage where there had never been cleavage before.

"Wow." She couldn't take her eyes off her chest. "Check it out," she murmured at her reflection, grinning lopsidedly. She looked...sexy. From neck to waist, that was.

Now for stockings. She fumbled with the garter belt and sheer black nylons, finally calling in frustration to her mother, "How do you attach these things?"

Candy came in, took one look at her and burst out laughing. "You're not seriously going to wear those," she exclaimed, pointing a long, glitter-polished nail toward Emma's white cotton briefs.

"Why not?"

"They don't exactly go with the rest of it."

"No one will see. Will you just please help me with these stockings? I can't figure out these little...*things* on the ends of these...*things*."

"Not unless you trade in those pediatric underpants for these," Candy said, holding up the black satin thong panties that matched the bra and garter belt.

"Mom, I don't have time for—"

"Look at yourself." Candy spun her around so that she faced the three-way mirror. Emma couldn't help but see her mother's point. The black garter belt over the white briefs looked... "Grotesque," Candy supplied.

"Okay," Emma muttered.

"I mean, what if you get in an accident?"

"I said okay!" Emma snatched the wisp of black satin from her mother. "Would you please turn around?"

"Honestly," Candy muttered, but she turned her back.

Emma squirmed when she got the panties on. "They don't cover anything. And they feel so—so..."

"You'll get used to 'em," Candy said, turning back around. "If I still had a butt like yours, I'd wear those and nothing else." She helped Emma connect the stockings to the garter belt and shimmy into the snug little skirt, which snapped up the front. "Wear these," she commanded, sliding black pumps with heels like ice picks onto Emma's stockinged feet. "You've got dynamite legs. Make the most of them."

"I can't walk in these."

"You'll get used to 'em."

Emma rolled her eyes. "Why should I have to *train* myself to wear uncomfortable clothes when I can wear jeans and a T-shirt and feel great?"

"Because you don't look like this in jeans and a T-shirt," Candy said, turning her around to look in the mirror once more.

"Holy cow."

"Ditto. Now let's fix that face of yours."

A WOLF WHISTLE greeted Emma the second she stepped from Zara's apartment into the hallway. "Looking good there, good-looking."

The rather redundant compliment, voiced in a Boston accent, had emerged from a burly man inserting a key in the apartment door next to Zara's. He was clad in sweatpants and a muscle T, with a gym bag slung over his shoulder, his upper body sculpted into a wedge of pure brawn. His head, Emma noted, was entirely, completely, blindingly bald; there wasn't a hair anywhere.

He surveyed her from head to foot, openly and without a shred of self-consciousness. From his expression of en-

thralled appreciation, he might have been checking out a
new car on the lot.

Emma muttered something polite and headed for the elevator.

"Hey, Zara!"

She turned around.

"Been working on the upper body. Check this out."
Dropping the gym bag, he struck a hulking pose, causing
all the muscles in his arms and torso to pop out in sharp relief. He looked like a balloon animal—a blondish gorilla, to
be exact, given the hair that blanketed him from the neck
down. "What do you think?" he gasped, his face purple,
the cords in his neck quivering with strain.

It's gonna blow! "Very nice," she said, edging away.

He straightened up and blinked at her. "Just nice?"

"No, you look..." *Simian.* "Virile. Extremely virile. Bye."
She pivoted on the pointy little shoes, which turned out to
be excellent for pivoting.

"Hey, Zara!"

She sighed and turned around.

"I traded in the old Porsche for a new one. White."

"I'm very happy for you." *Pivot.*

"Hey, Zara!"

Did all men act like slavering dogs around Zara? "Yes?"

He grinned and took a step toward her. "Have you seen
the new Van Damme flick?"

Emma took a step back. "No."

"I have. Twice. But I'll see it again, if you want to. Tonight, maybe?"

"Look, uh—" she glanced at the R. Harrington stenciled
onto his gym bag "—Mr. Harrington, I'm sorry, but—"

"What's this 'Mr. Harrington' business? Yesterday it was
'Ronald,' today it's 'Mr. Harrington'? This isn't good, Zara.
This is a step backward, when all I've been thinking

about—" he moved closer to her "—for months—" and closer "—is getting into your—" his gaze raked her "—heart."

"Look, Ronald—"

"Zara, you know how I feel about you."

Emma glanced at her watch. "Oops. Look at the time." She turned and ran.

"Would it kill you to give me a shot at you?" he called after her.

No, but it might hurt her. She punched the button for the elevator; it opened right away. "Sorry!" The doors closed. She caught her breath as she rode down to the lobby.

The doorman looked at her. He smiled politely as he held the door open, but his eyes flickered with something almost...primitive...as they gave her a swift and surreptitious once-over. Men on the street *turned* to give her that look. The cabdriver kept checking her out in the rearview mirror, which made her wonder whether it had been a mistake letting her mother do her makeup. Liquid eyeliner, for crying out loud. And her lips were baboon's-butt red. On the one hand, Emma felt like a fraud; if this wasn't false advertising, what was? On the other, she felt...

Powerful.

Emma smiled with heady feminine awareness as she paid the driver and negotiated the revolving glass door of the building that housed Zara's agency. So this was what it felt like to turn men on.

She stopped at the security desk, but the guard just grinned and waved her through. *Of course,* she thought as she covertly searched around for the elevators. *He thinks you're Zara. That's the point, right?*

Alone for a few blessed moments in the elevator, she closed her eyes and took a deep breath. She felt Zara's long, heavy earrings tickle her throat. She felt the lining of the leather suit, silky smooth against her nearly bare skin. She felt the weight of the garter belt on her hips and the tension in the little straps that held her stockings up. She felt her legs, stretched like a Barbie doll's as she stood on tiptoe in her Barbie shoes.

She felt *fabulous.*

She got out on the seventh floor and sucked in another deep breath before pushing open the glass door labeled Zara Sutcliffe Literary Agency.

"Zara!" The pert, redheaded receptionist leapt to her feet. "I thought you were still in Australia."

Emma rummaged in her mind for an appropriate response. "I came back early," she said, uninspired.

"So I see. Did you settle that business with Maxine Moore?"

The girl spoke about twice as fast as Emma could think, and in an abnormally high, squeaky voice. She again rummaged frantically. "I'm not sure."

The little redhead blinked at Emma's hair. "How'd your hair get so long all of a sudden?" A lightbulb went on in her eyes. "Is that a wig?" Before Emma could answer, she said, "Wow. It's a good one."

"Thanks—" Emma cut a glance to the nameplate on the reception desk "—Tina."

Tina grabbed a stack of pink phone-message slips and thrust them into her hand. "I put the ones that need to be returned on top."

Emma took the slips with unsteady fingers. "Great. I'll just go to my office now." *Wherever that is.*

Tina headed briskly up a hallway, rattling on about phone calls and lunches and meetings, sounding like an uncannily efficient Alvin the Chipmunk, and Emma followed her, thinking, *I don't believe I'm pulling this off.* At one point, the receptionist glanced behind her with a bemused expression and said, "New bag?"

Emma looked down at her big, overstuffed shoulder bag, which she'd made years ago out of antique quilt squares. It was homey and a little silly, and somewhat frayed around the edges, but it was her security blanket. In addition, it held an enormous collection of items she might need at any time, which she kept on a written list so she wouldn't ever forget anything:

1. Day Timer
2. Address book
3. Flashlight
4. First-aid kit
5. Miniature tool kit
6. Sewing kit
7. Sunglasses
8. Pepper spray
9. Snacks
10. Mineral water
11. Subway map
12. Current mystery
13. Mystery to read next...

And a couple dozen other things. These items being essential to her well-being and peace of mind, Emma had defied her mother and accessorized the hip little yellow suit with the decidedly unhip quilt bag.

"I called and canceled your appointments, like you told me to when you phoned." Tina hesitated in front of a door labeled Zara Sutcliffe. "Except for your three o'clock."

"That's all right." Emma opened the door to Zara's spacious, book-lined office and stepped inside. *Get rid of Tina, get the gun and get out.*

"I'm sorry." Tina's hands fluttered nervously. "He was en route when I tried to cancel, and I couldn't get in touch with him." She glanced into the office. "He's been waiting for a long—"

"It's okay, really." Emma, too preoccupied with her mission to absorb Tina's mile-a-minute yammering, slowly closed the door as the receptionist craned to peek through from the hallway.

"He's really mad," Tina whispered. "I'm really sorry."

"It's okay," Emma whispered back. "It's really okay." The door clicked shut. The air went out of her body, and she rested her forehead on the cool wood of the door. *I don't believe I'm doing this.*

She checked her watch. "Oh, boy." It was 4:40. She had twenty minutes to get the ray gun and get to SoHo. Wheeling around, she zeroed in on the oriental credenza next to the book-strewn desk and went to it, yanking open the double doors.

"Ah." There it was, propped up diagonally in the dark compartment, a gleaming chrome caricature of a deadly weapon. The ray gun that had whacked the Atomic Bride during her second and last celluloid incarnation was about the size and shape of a rifle, but sprouted a dizzying array of knobs, buttons and levers. Its futuristically fussy ornamentation gave it an art-deco look that had always appealed to Emma. Obviously, it appealed to someone else, too—someone willing to pay two million in cool, hard U.S. currency for it. There was something decidedly surreal about this whole transaction. What kind of a lunatic, regardless of how rich he was, would part with that kind of green for an old movie prop? It didn't make any sense, and that made her extremely uneasy.

Dumping her quilt bag on the desk, she hefted the ray gun in her hands, finding it to be remarkably heavy. The flared business end of the barrel housed several dozen little colored lightbulbs in concentric circles.

Turning, Emma lifted the ray gun to her shoulder and peered through the scope.

And saw a man. Sitting on a sofa in the corner with his feet on a coffee table and his hands in the air.

2

EMMA FROZE. *Think fast.* But she was incapable of thinking fast. Her mind seized up when she was under pressure, just as it was doing now.

"You want to aim that thing somewhere else, ma'am?" His deep, gravelly voice was seasoned with a down-home, Southern drawl. Sprawled as he was all over her sister's office furniture, she could see that he was long and tall, with the kind of rugged Marlboro Man looks you didn't expect to come across in Manhattan. His wire-rimmed glasses and the open book in his lap detracted slightly from the image, but the scuffed cowboy boots and worn corduroy jacket made up the difference. He looked vaguely familiar to her, but she knew she'd never met him.

"I said would you mind pointing that—" he squinted at the ray gun "—*weapon* in another direction?" Slowly lowering one hand, he slid off his glasses, folded them and tucked them beneath his jacket into a shirt pocket, all the while keeping his eyes trained on the ray gun. They must have been reading glasses, because he appeared to focus better on the gun without them; his increasingly mystified expression attested to that.

"I'm gonna get up slowly." Putting the book aside, he drew up his long, jean-clad legs and set his booted feet on the floor one after the other. "Just do me a favor and take your finger off the trigger."

Emma looked at the ray gun and then at the man rising

carefully from the sofa and stepping away from the coffee table, his hands still in the air. A little gasp of disbelieving laughter escaped her as she lowered the gun and pressed the trigger to show him it was just a harmless—

"Shit!" He ducked and rolled, then lunged for her. Grabbing her by the waist, he threw her to the carpeted floor, pinning her beneath him. She felt paralyzed with shock, overwhelmed by the weight of him on top of her, by his hands on her, prying open her fingers to wrest the gun from her grip. She gulped for air as he leapt to his feet.

Emma sat up on the floor, shaken and reeling. In her entire life, no one had ever handled her so roughly.

He stood in the corner by the sofa, inspecting the weapon in his hands with obvious puzzlement, his short brown hair in disarray. "What the Sam Hill...?"

"You didn't have to do that," she rasped as she tidied her hair with trembling fingers.

His gaze lit on her, traveling from her face to her chest, where it paused briefly, to her legs, where it lingered with frank interest. She recognized that look. She'd seen it in the eyes of the doorman and the cabdriver and a dozen other men since she'd transformed herself into Zara Sutcliffe.

Looking down at her legs, she saw that her skirt had ridden up in the scuffle, exposing the dark bands at the tops of her stockings as well as the little fasteners that connected them to the garter belt. Sucking in a breath, she tugged her skirt down. When she stole another glance at him, her cheeks stinging, she noted a trace of amusement in his eyes.

He stepped toward her and, holding the ray gun out of reach, extended a hand to help her up. She automatically shrank back before gathering her wits and gingerly accepting his offer. His hand was huge and rough, his grip strong. He brought her easily to her feet and then released her without taking his eyes off her face.

She took a step back and nodded toward the gun. "It's not a real one."

He regarded it with a dubious expression. "Not a real *what?*"

"Ray gun."

He cocked his head. "Ray gun." He turned the movie prop over in his hands, studying it from all angles. "This is a ray gun?"

"No—I told you. It's not a real one." Holding out her hand to take it, she said, "Do you mind?"

He impaled her with a look that made her shiver. "Oh, there's been a great deal to mind today," he drawled. "What, in particular, are you curious about my minding right now?"

His laid-back wrath gave Emma pause. "Would you...mind giving me the ray gun?"

He rested the gun on his shoulder and looked around. "What ray gun? I don't see any ray gun here."

Emma checked her watch—4:47—and looked up at him beseechingly. "Please—I have to be somewhere with that gun in thirteen minutes. This is really important."

He seemed suddenly more alert. "Oh, it's *important.*" He strode toward her. She stumbled back until she hit the desk; he stood over her, way too close. "Forgive me, Ms. Sutcliffe, I didn't understand you actually had *important* business today. I just thought you just had appointments you didn't mind missing. Like mine."

His eyes spat blue fire. Emma tried to tear her gaze away from them, but couldn't. "You're the three o'clock."

"Yes. I'm the three o'clock. I'm the three o'clock who flew all the way from nice, civilized Arkansas to this miserable, stinking seventh level of hell because—and this is the really funny part—you begged me to."

"I...I begged—"

"You weren't the only one, you know," he assured her, backing off a step. "Every agent in this godforsaken city put the moves on me after *Incision* made the *New York Times* list. But *you*, you were so all-fired persistent—stubborn as a fly."

"*Incision?*" she said. "The medical thriller? Omigod, you're Gage Foster!"

"You're just now figuring that out?"

That was why he looked so familiar, she realized. The jacket of the copy of *Incision* that she'd taken out of the library had featured a photo of him standing with two bloodhounds on the porch of a massive log house. She remembered thinking how craggily attractive he looked. "That was a great book!"

"Can't really see what all the fuss is about, myself."

"Wow! You're him. You're Gage Foster!"

THIS CONVERSATION was giving Gage Foster a pain behind his eyeballs.

"You did know I was coming," he said. "I'm your three o'clock—you said so yourself. You do remember all those months you pestered me to let you represent me? All those phone calls filled with promises about promotion campaigns and movie deals? You must have said 'seven figures' at least fifty times."

She just stared at him, like some big-eyed night thing caught in a flashlight. It was the same poleaxed expression she'd worn while she was holding that toy gun on him. Almost made him feel sorry for her.

"Here." He handed her back the gun. She closed her eyes in relief, cradling the weapon to her chest.

Now there was a sight, he thought, taking a mental picture of it for perusal later. She looked like a caricature of a Bad Girl from the Big City, which was entirely in keeping with what he'd been led to expect of Zara Sutcliffe. From what he'd heard, she was a real piece of work—a shark in her business dealings, the life of the party on her off-hours.

Her wardrobe was certainly Big City. That yellow leather fit her like the hide on a milk-fed calf. Then there were those nonstop legs ending in those prancey little Bad Girl shoes. That brief glimpse of garter belt had made him wish, for the first time since he was twelve, for the miracle of X-ray vision.

Turning her back on him, she reached for the big, funky shoulder bag she'd dumped on the desk. It looked like an old quilt all cut up and sewn back together again. Kind of goofy, but he liked it.

She tried to cram the ray gun into the bag, but it was obviously too full of other stuff. Peering over her shoulder, he saw a first-aid kit, a bottle of fancy-ass water, a flashlight....

"You plannin' on doin' some survival camping?" he asked her.

She didn't answer, just edged away from him. He edged closer, breathing in the scents of leather and baby powder. The baby powder surprised him. He would have expected some kind of musky, high-priced perfume.

"Take some of that stuff out," he suggested as she pawed urgently through the contents of her bag. "That's the only way that thing's gonna fit in there."

"I need this stuff."

"You *need* all of that? You haul that big passel of useless junk around with you—"

"It's not useless." She turned to face him, the picture of righteous indignation. "I need all of it." She sighed heavily. "Guess I'll just have to carry the gun."

"Openly?" He chuckled. "I don't know much about the local firearm statutes, but my guess is New York's finest will be on you like a cat on a copperhead before you can make it to the corner. Might mess up your schedule some."

Her elegant black eyebrows drew together as she contemplated that. She was pretty as hell despite all the makeup and that come-hither getup. He was partial to brown-eyed brunettes, and she was a good one, slender but curvy, with milky skin and delicate features—catlike eyes, high cheekbones, a nice, wide mouth and a cleft in her sharp little chin that he kept wanting to rub with his thumb.

Right. He'd best keep his thumbs off of Zara Sutcliffe. She was trouble. She'd already proven that, showing up an hour and forty minutes late for a meeting he'd flown all the way from Arkansas for. Come to think of it, she seemed to be fixing to stand him up altogether, without so much as a grudging "I'm sorry, but..." Where he came from, they'd run you out of town for that.

"About our appointment," he began, but she wasn't listening to him. She was staring at the coatrack near the door. One item hung on it—a shiny, gold vinyl raincoat. He kept an eye on her as she crossed to the rack, grabbed the coat and returned. Sweeping aside a pile of books on the desk, she spread out the coat with the inside facing up.

"Did you hear me?" he prodded. "I mean for you to keep that appointment you were so all-fired eager to set up." But she obviously *didn't* hear him, preoccupied as she was with sorting furiously through that big bag of hers.

"Ah." She pulled out a small plastic case and snapped it open. Gage saw two screwdrivers, a wrench, a pair of pliers....

"You know," he said, "this disorder probably has a name. You could get professional help for it."

She didn't acknowledge the comment as she withdrew a small roll of black electrical tape and a utility knife from the little toolbox. Positioning the ray gun lengthwise inside the vinyl coat, she proceeded to slice off sections of tape and press them down over the gun.

"Well, I'll be dipped," Gage muttered as she adhered the gun securely to the inner surface of the coat. When she was done, she hastily packed up, then donned the coat—beneath which the mock weapon was entirely invisible.

"I'm impressed," Gage admitted.

She shot him one of those smart-ass, *nyah-nyah* grins that should have looked obnoxious, but didn't. Not by a long shot. Her whole face ignited with pleasure in her own resourcefulness, like a little girl who'd done something clever beyond her years. It wasn't a look he would have expected to see on the face of Zara Sutcliffe, and it surprised him. Hell, it ambushed him. Snuck up and whopped him upside the head.

No, he told himself. *This is not going to happen. You don't like her. You like her damn handbag. That's not the same thing.*

She checked her watch. "I'm gonna be late," she moaned, clutching her bag and crossing to the door.

"Whoa." He overtook her as she reached for the knob. Gripping her by the shoulders, he spun her around and pressed her back against the door. "I don't think so, sweetheart."

She stilled momentarily, her eyes widening in evident panic. "I—I have to go." She tried to squirm out of his grip.

"Not until we've had our meeting."

She tried to sidestep him, but he held her tightly. "Let go of me," she said. "I can't think with you...with your hands on me like this."

He realized with astonishment that she was trembling—not how he would have expected Zara Sutcliffe to react to a man's touch. Not only was she a divorcée, but the tabloids were full of pictures of her on the arms of Hollywood big shots.

Nevertheless, he eased off a bit, releasing her shoulders, but standing close enough that he could stop her if she tried to make a run for it. "I didn't come all the way from Arkansas for nothing," he said. "You made an appointment, and you're damn well going to keep it." He shook his head in frustration. "I never swear in front of women. Look what you've driven me to, dammit."

"Look." She glanced at her watch again and talked fast. "I have six minutes left. I'm sorry about the appointment. It was supposed to be canceled. That girl, Tina, she made phone calls this morning—"

"I was in the air this morning. Why couldn't she have called me yesterday, before I went to the trouble of flying all the way up here?"

"I don't—"

"I don't, either," he said. "But now that we're both here, we can have our meeting."

"But I have to be—"

"You have to be somewhere in six minutes. Cancel *that* appointment."

"I can't. There's no way!" Her chin began to wobble.

"Don't." He pressed his thumb in the indentation in her chin, just as he'd been wanting to do.

Damn. He was going to cave in. He felt it in his bones. *Damn, damn and double damn.*

Gage was a sucker for vulnerable women, always had been. It was all his mother's fault. She never should have convinced him, after he'd had the temerity to return Evil Evelyn Platt's roundhouse punch in the second grade, that it was his duty as a gentleman to protect the weaker sex— he was supposed to take it, but never even dream of dishing it out. He'd long since realized that females weren't weaker, just smarter, but he couldn't seem to rein in this knee-jerk compulsion he had to take care of them. All of them.

Even a barracuda like Zara Sutcliffe.

He was about to tell her she'd won, and he'd come back and meet with her tomorrow, because he wasn't flying back until the day after, but before he could, she said, "This has gone on too long. I've got to tell you the truth."

Gage's ears tickled at the word *truth*.

She drew in a shaky breath and looked everywhere but at his eyes. "I'm not Zara Sutcliffe."

He stared at the top of her head. "Pardon me?"

"I'm her twin sister, Emma, and I know it sounds crazy, but I had to pretend to be Zara, and now everything's going wrong," she blurted out in a rush. "And I have to go, I *have* to. You have to let me go, please." She raised those choco-latey cat eyes to his imploringly. "Please."

"Oh, I don't think so," he said, outrage moving in quickly to replace any misguided urge he may have had to play the Southern gentleman in this particular scenario. "You just made your fatal error, sweetheart—tryin' to slither out of this with a tale like that. If there's any one thing that gets my boxers into a twist, it's being lied to."

"B-but I'm not lying," she stammered. "I'm really Zara's twin—"

He took her by the arm and pulled her away from the door, then opened it and yelled, "Tina!" down the hall.

The receptionist materialized in the open doorway. "Uh, may I help you, sir?"

"Who is this?" he asked, tilting his head toward the shiv-ering woman in his grip.

Tina hesitated, her eyes darting back and forth between them.

"It's not a trick question," he said.

"That's Zara Sutcliffe." Tina zapped a look toward her boss, as if to say, *What's going on here?*

"Thank you," he said, in a tone of dismissal. She turned and left, shaking her head.

Zara eyed the open doorway.

"Don't even think about it." Gage tightened his grip on her arm. "We're gonna have our meeting now."

"Let me reschedule you. Please!"

"'Fraid not. You don't exactly have a sterling track record for keeping appointments."

"I'll keep this one!"

"Prove it."

"How?"

He allowed himself a mean-spirited little smile. "By making the appointment for—" he checked his own watch "—4:58 and keeping it now."

"It's 4:58?" She actually grew pale, and for a second there he thought she might faint smooth away. But then a sense of calm seemed to overtake her. He felt her relax beneath his grasp, and he loosened it experimentally. She didn't move. "You win," she said. "We'll have our meeting now."

"Hallelujah," Gage said, pleasure in his victory warring with suspicion.

She extended her free arm toward her desk. "Any objection to sitting down for this, or would you prefer to back me against the door again? Or maybe throw me to the floor?"

Not trusting himself to answer that one, he released her and followed her across the room, admiring the way her round little bottom stretched that yellow leather. She was tall in those mile-high heels, but without them she'd be maybe five-six. She had the legs of a Rockette, though, long and luscious.

He sat where she pointed, a black leather chair facing her desk.

"I'm sorry we started things off on the wrong foot," she said smoothly, her transformation to coolheaded business-woman eerily thorough. "It was all my fault and I apologize."

"It's perfectly all right," he mumbled, trained since infancy to accept apologies graciously, even when the situation was most decidedly not perfectly all right, and even if he had a pretty good idea she was up to something.

"I do have some promotion ideas I want to run past you," she said, circling the desk and pulling out her chair. "And if you haven't thought about selling to Hollywood, this is the time to talk about that. In my opinion, seven figures is not unrealistic." She picked up one of the books that littered her desk and handed it to him. "This author got a million five for the movie rights." She winced as she started to sit. Opening up the gold raincoat, she chuckled at the ray gun taped inside. "Excuse me."

Shrugging off the coat, she crossed behind him to the coatrack. Gage looked at the book she'd handed him: *Low-fat Recipes from the Great Chefs.* He leafed through the pages. It was a cookbook. Who'd pay a million five for movie rights to—

He swung around in his chair. The coat stand was empty. The door stood open.

"Shoot!" Hurling the book to the floor, he bolted up from his chair and sprinted out of the room, skidding on the marble floor of the hallway.

"Where'd she go?" he barked at the receptionist.

Tina glanced toward the glass door, beyond which the elevator doors were sliding shut.

"Stairs!" he shouted. "Are there stairs?"

She pointed mutely. Gage raced down seven flights two

steps at a time and hurtled outside, into the mayhem of rush hour in Manhattan. The sidewalk was a moving river of pedestrians—a river that had, for all intents and purposes, swallowed Zara Sutcliffe whole. Figuring she might try to hail a cab, he muscled his way to the corner, only to find the intersection jammed solid with bumper-to-bumper vehicles snared in a two-way standstill. Voices bellowed an international chorus of profanity as car horns trumpeted in accompaniment. There were cabs in that throng, but none of them was going anywhere. If Zara Sutcliffe meant to get to that precious appointment of hers, she'd either have to walk or...

There she was, a flash of gold among a group of people snaking their way between the gridlocked cars to get to the other side of the street. Peering at the opposite corner, he saw her obvious destination—a subway stairwell, into which dozens of bodies were descending as one.

Gage groaned. Everything he despised about this town—the crime, the filth, the smells, the noise—was superconcentrated once you got underground. Whenever he came to New York—which, thankfully, wasn't that often—he somehow managed to get sucked down into the subway system, and every time, he promised himself it wouldn't happen again.

She's not worth it, he told himself as he watched the glimmer of gold vinyl join the stream of humanity pouring into the stairwell. *Count your losses and walk away.*

EMMA CHECKED HER WATCH for the hundredth time that day as she weaved through the afternoon crowd on the subway platform. It was twelve minutes after five. She was late. Mac had probably left his office in SoHo, thinking he was being stood up. If only Gage Foster had let **her** go sooner. Now the deal was blown, and she'd have to tell her sister, and their mother would live with them forever, and people were bumping into her, and she wasn't sure which train to take anyway, and she couldn't breathe down here, and she wished she were dead.

From within the milling throng, she noticed a figure moving toward her with what looked like a sense of purpose—an oddity in an environment in which everyone studiously ignored everyone else. Then she recognized him, having seen him a couple of minutes ago, hanging around outside Zara's office building. From all appearances, he was a bum. That was probably a politically incorrect term, but she didn't know any other word for a guy with long, scraggly hair who wore about seven layers of shabby clothes and one layer of what looked like plain old dirt.

He'd started to approach her up on the sidewalk as she surveyed the traffic jam that had taken all the cabs out of commission. Then she'd spied the subway entrance across the street and made a beeline for it. She thought she'd shaken him off—strangers made her nervous, and this stranger made her very nervous—but here he was again, looking oddly determined as he strode toward her.

He probably wanted money, but Emma had one ten-dollar bill in her wallet, and she wasn't about to give it away. She tried to remember how much she had in change, but the whole station was vibrating with the approach of a train through the tunnel and she couldn't think.

As the bum closed in on her, she saw that he had his eyes trained on her shoulder bag.

Uh-oh. Tightening her grip on the bag, Emma backed up fast through the swarm of commuters. She shouldn't have let herself look so lost and vulnerable. Criminals preyed on the weak; that's why this guy had picked her to rip off, out of the hundreds of other candidates.

She stopped when the crowd thinned out. Glancing behind her, she found she was at the edge of the platform. When she looked back around, the bum was right there, reaching for her bag. He tore it away from her with one hard yank. "No!" she screamed.

He met her gaze, his eyes glowing in his filthy face.

Two horn blasts made her jump. An express train roared into the station.

The purse snatcher smiled.

And then he pushed her off the platform.

3

EMMA CLAWED AT THE AIR as she toppled over, her scream absorbed by the thunder of the oncoming train. Pain warred with panic as she landed on the tracks. Thank God, she'd missed the third rail.

Headlights bore down on her. Could she hoist herself up onto the platform? She clambered to her feet as the train barreled toward her, its horn blaring once, twice, three times.

There's not enough time. This is it.

Someone else landed heavily on the tracks and pushed her to her knees. For an insane moment she thought it was the purse snatcher, but when she looked up she saw...*Gage Foster?*

He's crazy! She struggled to rise, but he shoved her roughly into a narrow recess beneath the platform that she hadn't seen. He came in after her, banding his arms around her and crushing her against the concrete wall as a deafening rumble filled her ears and racked her body.

They both shook as the train stormed through the station, its wheels mere inches away. She couldn't see a thing, but she could smell hot metal and sizzling electricity.

His arms tightened around her, one hand cupping her head against his shoulder, the other gripping her waist beneath the raincoat. Her heart felt as if it might explode right through her chest. She felt his mouth moving against her hair and realized he was speaking to her, although his words were swallowed up by the din that enveloped them. There was something surreal about somebody *talking* under these circumstances, yet she found the fact that he could do so, and that he wanted to do so, strangely comforting. She strained to hear his words, but they were lost in the metallic scream that reverberated all around them.

This can't be happening, she thought wildly. *Things like this don't happen to me.*

The great roar receded; air rushed into their little niche. The train was leaving the station, she realized, although she couldn't seem to move, even to the extent of opening her eyes. Gage rubbed her back in a soothing, circular rhythm. She still felt the movement of his lips against her hair, and now she could feel his warm breath as well, ruffling the unruly strands.

"It's all right, now," he murmured. "Everything's going to be all right...."

Her legs were tangled with his, her hands gripping his corduroy jacket. She tried to unclench them, but couldn't.

"It's all over. You're fine. Everything's okay...."

Yeah, everything's just dandy. Some lunatic snatched my bag and pushed me into the path of an oncoming train, and now I'm suffering from hysterical paralysis and they're going to have to separate me from you surgically, but hey! That's life in the big city.

"Are you laughing?" he asked.

Even as she shook her head, she realized that she *was* laughing. She was also perilously close to tears. But she'd moved! Progress!

"Come on, sweetheart." He eased away from her fractionally and gently pried her fingers loose from his jacket. "Let's get topside before another train comes."

"Another..." The threat of being trapped in that cranny by another train pumped an energizing jolt of adrenaline through Emma. She pushed against him. "Move! What are you waiting for?"

Chuckling, he rolled away, and she scrambled out after him. The crowd on the platform cheered as he helped her to stand.

A giant clone of Shaquille O'Neal lifted her up and set her carefully on her feet; she teetered, oddly off balance. "You all right, miss?" He slid a cell phone out of his backpack, flipped it open and punched out 911.

"I..." Emma looked down at herself. The gold raincoat was soot smudged, although she still felt the weight of the ray gun taped inside, so she knew it hadn't gotten dislodged. Her black stockings were a network of runs. Both knees were scraped, one pretty badly, but she felt no pain. "I'm missing a shoe." That's why she'd felt off balance. One foot remained miraculously stiletto heeled; the other was bare.

"Here you go." Gage, still standing on the track, tossed the missing shoe onto the platform, then planted his hands on the edge and vaulted himself up, with remarkable grace. Squatting down, and taking the shoe in one hand, he grasped her ankle. His fingers felt warm through the taut nylon of her stocking. "Lift your foot."

She did, but had to lean over and hold on to his shoulders for balance. Cradling her foot, he slipped the shoe on, wriggling it into place. The action felt so...intimate that for a moment she couldn't breathe.

Get a grip, Emma. He's just putting on your shoe. And she was just the world's most repressed virgin, to be unnerved by it.

She lowered the foot and released his shoulders, but her legs still wobbled; her knees didn't seem to be doing their job very well just now.

Gage glided his hand from her ankle to her calf and in-

spected her knees, and then looked up at her, his blue eyes
incandescent in the dismal subway station. "You cryin'?"

"No," she sniffed, as hot tears trickled down her face.

"Yes you are." He stood, looking concerned and more
than a little perplexed, as if it had never before occurred to
him that the human eye could produce tears, and now that
he was faced with that reality, he was at a complete loss as
to how to proceed. Patting all his jacket pockets, one after
the other, he said, "Now, that's enough of that."

"Okay," she replied dutifully in a wet, quavering voice.

"Come on, now." Finally producing a folded white
handkerchief, he blotted her cheeks, then rubbed firmly.
"At least all that black stuff's getting washed off."

Black stuff? Did he mean soot or...

Emma groaned as her mind's eye conjured up a picture
of herself, eyeliner and mascara coursing down her face in
inky rivulets, to be mopped up by a nonplussed but solici-
tous Gage Foster. Could her humiliation be more complete?

Gage frowned in concentration as he deep-sixed the eye
makeup Emma's mother had so painstakingly applied.
Then he paused, his gaze fixed on her mouth. With a dazed
sense of unreality she watched him fold the handkerchief
over to expose a clean spot, which he wiped over her lips. It
came away streaked with crimson. He folded and wiped
again, then again, until all traces of her lipstick—or rather,
Zara's lipstick—were eradicated.

And then he smiled, first at her lips and then at her
eyes—a slow, sweet smile, as if he were seeing her for the
very first time. "That's better," he said, and shoved the
handkerchief back in his pocket.

"I saw the guy who did it," Shaq offered.

"Yeah, so did I," Gage said, "from the back." He scanned
the crowd. "I doubt I'd even know him if I saw him again."

"I'd recognize him anywhere," Emma said. "His eyes, they were...wolf's eyes."

"Uh-huh." Gage rubbed the back of his neck. "Think you can be any more specific?"

"Gold, they were golden. And...savage. When I was a kid, my father had this painting of a wolf in his den. Its eyes used to give me the creeps big-time." John Sutcliffe had liked wolves, creatures as cold-blooded and pitiless as himself.

"That was quick," said Shaq as two men in dark blue uniforms approached them through the milling onlookers, who pointed in her direction.

"You the one ended up on the tracks?" asked the first, an extremely tall man with a hound-dog face who made her think of Muldoon from the old *Car 54* series. His fireplug partner completed the image: Toody and Muldoon. Emma wondered if they'd been paired up deliberately for comic effect.

At some point during her muddled deliberations, the two cops introduced themselves as officers from Transit Borough One, or maybe it was Transit *Bureau* One; nothing seemed to be registering quite right. She couldn't remember their names five seconds after they'd said them. Her brain appeared to be operating with a kind of underwater torpidity. She wondered if this was how it felt to be drunk or stoned. *Nah. Who'd go out of their way to feel like this?*

The transit cops noted Shaq's description of the assailant and dismissed him. Toody questioned Gage, while Muldoon led Emma some distance away, to a bench in a relatively quiet corner of the platform. She sat down and wrapped her arms around herself. The cop produced a notepad and flipped it open.

"We came soon as we heard the long short," said Muldoon, after taking her name and address.

Emma blinked at him. "The long..."

"It's a series of three blasts from the motorman's horn," he explained. "He saw you get pushed onto the tracks and gave the signal."

"Oh." *The long short?* Emma felt as if she were wading through one of those disturbing dreams where a vague sense of wrongness keeps intruding on otherwise normal events.

"You hurt?" he asked, giving her the once-over and squinting at her ravaged knees. "You need to go to the hospital?"

She shook her head violently. She hated hospitals, with their poking and prodding and lack of privacy. All those strangers, touching her. "No, it's just a couple of skinned knees."

"You could have other injuries you don't know about yet. Sometimes things don't show up till later. Happened to my sister, after she cracked up her car on the Whitestone Bridge. She walked away feeling fine. That night she goes to take out the garbage and faints dead away. Turned out she had a concussion, two cracked ribs, whiplash—"

"I'm okay, really."

"You should let me call for an ambulance, just to check you out and make sure everything's okay."

"No, really, I'm fine." Except that her throat felt as if it had been sandblasted; she must have screamed at some point, although she couldn't remember it.

"Have it your way," he conceded grudgingly. "But you pay attention. If you start getting any funny aches or pains, you hightail it to the emergency room pronto."

She promised that she would.

"Do you know the perpetrator?" asked Muldoon, scratching behind his ear with his pen.

"Know him?" Emma shook her head. "No, he was

just...you know. A bum. Long, scraggly hair. Ratty clothes. He was filthy."

"Probably a junkie." He wrote something down. "You sure you never met him before?"

"No. I just moved here."

At Muldoon's urging, Emma described the assailant in as much detail as she could summon up. The only thing she remembered vividly was his eyes.

She related the entire encounter: how she'd seen the man for the first time outside Zara's building, and then on the platform, and then how he'd snatched her bag and pushed her. No, she didn't notice which way he went after that; she was too busy getting ready to die.

The cops' supervisor, a uniformed clone of Marlon Brando in his hair-raising *Apocalypse Now* incarnation, showed up with his own notebook and asked her all the same questions. Gage and Toody joined them. Marlon had Gage repeat in detail his witnessing of the crime. While he was going over it all again, Emma started to shake.

It wasn't so much a shivering as a sort of slow-motion trembling. Her arms and legs, and then her whole body, began to shudder uncontrollably. She willed it to stop, but it just got worse. She had no command whatsoever over her body; it had its own agenda.

By the time the cops had finished with Gage and returned their attention to her, still sitting with her arms locked around herself, she was quaking from head to toe. Her heart raced; her breath came in pants. Her stomach was a red-hot knot inside her, but the rest of her felt chilled to the bone.

All the men gaped at her, except for Gage, who whipped off his jacket and draped it over her, then sat next to her on the bench and rubbed her back and arms through the corduroy and vinyl and leather. His touch should have unnerved her, but instead it actually made her feel safer...comforted. "Easy, now. It's just adrenaline."

"A-adrenaline?"

"A delayed reaction to a life-threatening situation—very common. Your brain perceived a crisis and started hollerin' at your adrenal glands to pump out epinephrine—that's adrenaline—and norepinephrine, or noradrenal—"

"H-h-how do you know a-all th-th—"

He grinned in a bemused way. "They made me learn that kind of stuff before they let me start cuttin' folks open."

She stared at him for a moment, her teeth chattering, while she tried to remember details of the author's bio from the *Incision* jacket, which she'd hastily skimmed. "Y-you're a s-s-surgeon."

The grin faded; the light went out of his eyes. "Used to be."

"That's about it, Ms. Sutcliffe," Marlon said without looking up from his notepad. "We'll try and find the creep who did this to you, and recover your bag, but I gotta be honest with you—it's a long shot. Slimeballs like that have a way of disappearing pretty good once they hit the street."

Emma nodded dejectedly. "I h-had everything in that bag."

Gage grunted. "I'd like to see the look on that clown's face when he starts wadin' through all that... Wait a minute. Your wallet was in there, right? And your house keys?"

"Sure."

Gage turned to Marlon. "This guy's got her address and the keys to her house."

The supervisor glanced up at her from his notepad. "Yeah, I was gonna say, it's probably a good idea if you don't go home."

Don't go home? Where else was she supposed to go?

"Not till you can get the locks changed," he amended. "And I wouldn't try to arrange that till tomorrow. I definitely wouldn't go anywhere near there this evening, unless you're in the mood to run into this guy again."

"You're kidding," she groaned.

Marlon shrugged and slid his notebook into the back pocket of his uniform. "Could be this fella figures this'd be a good time to rip you off. You might show up at your house to find him still there. We already know he's a homicidal lunatic. I don't want to think about you being trapped in a house with him. What we'll do is have the Queens police patrol your neighborhood. If he makes an appearance, we might have a chance of catching him."

"This kind of thing never happened to me in Maine," she murmured.

"Welcome to the Big Apple," Gage said.

"You can call a locksmith tomorrow," Marlon said. "In the meantime, do you have anyplace you can go? Someplace you can spend the night?"

"Spend the night?"

"Friends you can stay with?" Gage prompted.

Friends? She'd only just moved here. She didn't know a soul in New York, with the exception of Zara and her mother. She envisioned showing up at Zara's apartment and trying to explain to her mom what she was doing there, battered and bruised and with the ray gun taped inside her raincoat. Candy wasn't supposed to know about the sale; she'd be appalled—and hurt—that they'd gone behind her back. Zara would go ballistic.

Zara! What if she called while Emma was at her place? What was Emma supposed to say? She'd just blown a two-million-dollar sale. Granted, she had excuses out the wazoo, but two million bucks was two million bucks, and somehow she doubted her sister would view her failure to consummate this deal with anything approaching equanimity. No, she wasn't eager to confront either her mother or her sister anytime soon.

"No," Emma said, "there's no one I can stay with." Her trembling, which had diminished some, now reasserted itself.

"No one?" Gage said incredulously. "That can't be possible."

"There's no one I can stay with," she repeated firmly, her voice cracking. *For heaven's sake, don't start crying again; this is embarrassing enough.* "No one."

Gage regarded her curiously, then sighed. "I can get you a hotel room."

She nodded, then shook her head. "I have no money, no credit cards. It was all in my bag."

He waved a dismissive hand. "I'll pay for it."

"I couldn't accept that."

Muldoon shook his hound-dog head. "I don't like the idea of it, anyway. She shouldn't stay alone, not after what she's been through. She could be hurt bad and not know it. Somebody should be there to keep an eye on her."

Gage rubbed his chin and studied the concrete platform as if it were suddenly fascinating. "You, uh...you could stay with me tonight," he said, without looking at her.

"You?"

He cleared his throat and hesitantly met her gaze. "Sure, I mean...I've got a room at the Plaza. It's...well, right now it's got just the one bed, but I can switch it for a room with two doubles."

Separate beds. All fine and dandy, except Emma had never spent the night in the same room with a man in her life, and now she was supposed to sleep in close proximity to a near-total stranger?

"I know you don't know me very well," Gage continued,

"but it doesn't sound like you've got a whole lot of options. And if you're worried about your virtue," he added, his good-ol'-boy drawl kicking into overdrive, "my momma brung me up to keep my hands to myself 'less I asked pretty please first."

A smile yanked at the corner of her mouth, despite her apprehension.

"Plus which," Muldoon added, "he's a doctor, isn't that right?"

A muscle leapt in Gage's jaw. "Ex-doctor."

"He can keep an eye out for you," the cop noted cheerfully, then clapped his hands together. "Sound like a plan?"

Toody, Muldoon, Marlon and Gage stared raptly at her, waiting for her answer.

SOME PLAN, thought Gage Foster as the cab he'd flagged down wove through traffic at about Mach 2, tossing its two passengers around like rag dolls. *And it was my idea. Why did I have to volunteer to be the knight in shining armor?*

He stole glances at Zara Sutcliffe, sitting stiffly with one white-knuckled fist clutching the door handle, the other gripping the back of the driver's seat. For a fleeting moment a shaft of late afternoon sunlight played over her face, firing up the bronze in her eyes and lighting up her porcelain skin from within.

Whoa there, partner. Bronze? Porcelain? Best you keep your eyes on the trail. She was Trouble with a capital T. Big-time trouble. She'd proven that in spades.

Nevertheless, he snatched another quick peek as she gazed pensively out the side window at the buildings and cars and people streaking by. That ol' damsel-in-distress thing always undid him. Whenever he encountered a woman in need, he felt a profound moral obligation to slay whatever dragons had to be slain in order to make things right again. At the same time, there was something about this particular damsel's aura of loopy guilelessness that made him want to pop all the snaps on that hot little yellow getup of hers and find out what was underneath.

Guileless? Zara Sutcliffe?

Well...as a matter of fact, yes. Stripped as she was of all the war paint and attitude, she struck him as a different woman entirely from the one he'd thought he'd be dealing with. Beneath that slick facade lurked a sort of earnest artlessness he found all too compelling.

He thought about that big, silly, strangely appealing bag of hers—so incongruous in the possession of the Glamourpuss Dealmaker he'd expected. It seemed there was more to her than met the eye. There was apparently a different, more ingenuous, more *real* Zara that she preferred to keep under wraps.

The cab abruptly turned a corner, jostling them both. Gage put a hand out to steady himself, brushed her leg and apologized automatically. She caught her lower lip between her teeth and held it there, just for a second, then let it go. Her ripe mouth was suddenly suffused with a hot bloom of color that beat the pants off that Crayola red she'd had on before. He wondered if her lips would feel hot to the touch if he just—

Man, you are just consumed with dumb-ass. Don't even think about this.

She fidgeted on the seat, her eyes alert and wary as she glanced at him, then abruptly looked away. He knew their little adventure in the subway station had unnerved her badly—how could it not?—but he sensed a different and deeper disquiet in her. It had to do with him; that was clear as Mississippi bottom mud. Every time he touched her—and he seemed to be having a hellaciously hard time keeping his paws off her—she went real still and wide-eyed, like a barn kitten that's never been petted. Except this was Zara Sutcliffe. If the tabloids had it right, every stud duck in New York and L.A. was lining up to stroke her fur. What was it about him in particular that made her so nervous?

She noticed him looking at her, and held his gaze for a breathless nanosecond before looking away.

But then she looked back.

And smiled.

Ah. He returned her smile, new and intriguing possibilities crawling out from somewhere deep within his sensory cortex and marching up to the front door of his frontal lobes, candy and flowers in hand, grinning with goofy anticipation. *She likes you. That's why she's nervous around you. And you like...her handbag. You even like* her *a little. Go ahead—ask pretty please and see what she says.*

She leaned toward him, just slightly.

Yes!

"Gage, I...want to thank you. For jumping down on the tracks like that."

He cleared his throat. "You're welcome."

"You saved my life," she said with quiet sincerity.

He poured a little syrup on the drawl and went for an engaging grin. "My pleasure, ma'am."

"Really, it was incredibly brave of you, and selfless, and I can't believe you did it. You have no idea how grateful I am."

Her eyes were huge and had darkened to polished ebony. It was the result, he saw, of dilated pupils—the autonomic nervous system's telltale indication of interest, emotional excitement...and sometimes sexual arousal. He was beginning to suspect that she might be very grateful, indeed.

Which was all well and good. Extremely good, in fact.

Except for that little problem of mixing business and pleasure, never a bright idea, but particularly dumb in this situation. A quick, uncomplicated fling with a beautiful woman in tight yellow leather held a certain inescapable appeal to him right at present; if nothing else, it would salvage what was turning into a fairly pointless—not to mention life-threatening—excursion to his all-time least-favorite city. The fly in the ointment was this particular beautiful woman's expectation of signing him on as a client. Somehow he suspected that a fling with his own agent was unlikely to turn out either quick or uncomplicated. On the contrary, there was every chance it would result in a disaster of titanic proportions, both personally and professionally.

He'd never been fond of titanic disasters.

She crossed her legs—crossed *toward* him, if you paid any heed to that body-language business, which he never had before, but that didn't mean there wasn't a grain of truth in it—which caused the gold plastic raincoat to part and the yellow leather skirt to hitch up on her Rockette thighs, revealing just the narrowest little sliver of black band at the top of her mangled left stocking.

"Did you say something?" she asked.

"No, I just..." *Moaned.* "Cleared my throat."

Gage regarded the tempting little strip of black stocking thoughtfully as he weighed his options in regard to the ever-more-provocative Zara Sutcliffe. The way he saw it, he had two decent and ethical choices. He could avoid such an assignation outright. Or...he could simply eliminate the conflict with a little...preventive medicine, as it were. He could tell her up front—now, before anything happened—the truth: that he had no intention of taking her on as his agent.

At one point, while she was sweet-talking him over the

phone about megadeals and movie sales and displays in every superstore, he'd been tempted. But now, after seeing her in action, no way would he put his career in her hands. He didn't know much about Zara Sutcliffe, but he knew in his bones she was no businesswoman. A surprisingly charming girl underneath it all, and way too sexy for her own good, but no businesswoman. How she'd gotten this far was a mystery to him.

The solution, therefore, was to break it to her, as kindly as possible, that she didn't have a chance in hell of becoming his agent. He'd have to do it eventually; he might as well bite the bullet and do it now, to her face, rather than taking the chickenshit approach and calling her when he got back to Arkansas. She wouldn't be happy about it. *Incision* continued to astound the industry with its sales figures, and if the advance reviews for his upcoming *Open Heart* were any indication, it would do as well or better. An agent's cut of his book royalties alone would rack up into the six figures, and if you added movies on top of it, well...you could kind of understand the feeding frenzy that had surrounded him for the past few months, as agents wooed him shamelessly.

The hungriest shark in the sea—the most doggedly eager—had been Zara Sutcliffe. She'd spent more time, money and energy courting him than had anyone else. His decision not to go with her—especially on the heels of the day's traumatic events—could upset her. He hoped she wouldn't cry again. He prided himself on never having been the cause of a woman's tears, and he'd hate to start with this woman, after everything she'd been through.

He rehearsed in his mind the diplomatic words he'd use. He'd tell her he didn't want her harboring any misconceptions—that he meant no offense, but he simply wasn't interested in her as an agent. Not that she wasn't a swell human being and all, but business was business. Surely they could still be friends. After all, he found her very attractive as a person. Very attractive.

Filled with heady confidence, he almost smiled before it occurred to him that his little speech would be better served with a more sober expression. "Zara, in the interest of complete honesty, there's something I'd like to get clear between us."

She perked up. "Honesty?"

"Yes. I don't want there to be any misconceptions between us."

"Neither do I." She sat up straighter, suddenly animated. "There's something I need to tell you, too, and you've got to listen to me this time."

Her intensity took him aback. "All right. You go first."

She leaned toward him, and he breathed in her baby-powder scent. "What I told you before, about being Zara's twin sister?"

He nodded carefully.

"It's true. My name is Emma Sutcliffe. You have to believe me."

He groaned and sank back into the seat. "This isn't multiple-personality disorder, is it? My hotel room isn't big enough for more than two of us."

She dragged a hand through her disheveled hair. "Why won't you believe me?"

"Look, Zara—"

"Emma."

"Your own receptionist identified you, all right? And what was all that talk about Hollywood and seven figures back at your office? You yourself admitted you were Zara Sutcliffe."

"I...well, I lied. Then. For a reason. Now I'm telling the truth."

"Uh-huh. Look, Zara, I don't know what you're trying to pull off here, but—"

"Pull off?" She put on a fairly credible display of indignation. Clearly, she wanted desperately for him to believe her, and that desperation roused his protective instinct, an instinct he'd just have to try and ignore in the present circumstance. She was pulling one over on him, he reminded himself; this was a game to her, in which she made up the rules as she went along. "I'm telling you the truth here!" Her voice wobbled just like the real thing. "All I want is for you to believe me."

He nodded slowly, fighting his urge to cave in. "I think I know what's going on here. You're pretty nervy, I'll give you that. And resourceful. You figure with everything you've put me through today, starting with the appointment you forgot about, that you've blown any chance you might have had of signing me on. *But!* If you can convince me you're not Zara Sutcliffe at all, that you're her...evil twin or whatever—"

"I'm the good twin," she informed him sullenly.

"Says you. If you can actually pull this masquerade off, I won't be mad at Zara Sutcliffe at all. If anything, I'll be mad at her twin, and she—or rather, you—will still have a chance to represent The Next Grisham."

Her jaw actually dropped. "Is that what they're calling you?"

"Don't be impressed. You, of all people, should know media hype when you smell it."

"I'm impressed anyway. But your theory is ludicrous. What kind of flake would pretend to be her *twin* just to pull off some stupid..." Frowning in a sheepish way, she turned and looked out the window. "Deal," she finished in a small voice.

"What kind of flake would walk the streets of New York

with a ray gun taped inside her raincoat? I don't know. You tell me."

With a lengthy sigh, she slumped forward and rested her head in her hands. "I'm Emma Sutcliffe. I swear it."

"Prove it." He seemed to be saying that a lot.

"How?"

"A driver's license would do nicely."

"It's in my bag. That creep has it now."

"I accept all major credit cards."

"They're in there, too, as you're well aware. Everything is."

"Business cards?"

"I have some. They're at home. Look." She gazed up at him with big, tragic eyes. "If I had **any** of that stuff on me, I could prove it to you, but I don't. You'll just have to take it on faith. You'll just have to believe me."

A burst of grim laughter escaped him. "Sorry, sweetheart, but that's a bad habit I broke a long time ago."

"What is?"

"Believing."

"In anything?"

"In people. In what they tell you and who they make themselves out to be. The way I see it, a fella's best off just ignoring what most folks have to say about themselves."

She looked genuinely interested and genuinely shocked. "Why?"

"People lie about themselves constantly. They lie about other stuff, too, if they think it'll get 'em what they want in life. The vast majority of humankind is inherently dishonest—completely lacking in integrity—and there's just nothing to be done about it but steer clear of 'em and look after your own interests."

"That's pretty cynical."

"What it is is realistic."

"And you're some kind of paragon of honesty, I suppose."

"Compared to most folks I've met in this world, yes, I guess I am. I happen to think honor and honesty mean something—it's how I was brought up. I was also brought up to expect others to be the same, but that's where my parents failed me. They were just setting me up for disappointment."

The cab swung sharply, lurching to a stop that left them in a jumbled heap in the corner where the back seat met the left-hand door. "Plaza," the cabbie announced, and clicked off the meter.

Gage levered himself off Zara, his hands braced on the seat back and door to either side of her, but he didn't move away; he wanted her complete attention. "I want to get this settled before we go in there." He nodded toward the archaically elegant facade of the building in front of which they were parked. "I'm sorry, but I've had a long, tiring, preternaturally frustrating day, and I'm in no mood whatsoever to be stuck in a hotel room with someone who's puttin' on her own little one-woman play. So, what do you say? You willin' to drop the act so we can get along?"

"Hey, buddy!" the driver barked. "That'll be seven-fifty."

Gage moved infinitesimally closer to Zara and lowered his voice just a hair. "That's all I want. Just to get along."

"Nothing I can say will convince you?"

He shook his head.

She bit that full bottom lip again. She had just about the sexiest mouth he'd ever laid his two eyes on. He reminded himself that he still hadn't broken it to her that she was out of the running as his agent; he'd have to take care of that little piece of business at the first opportunity. Once that was settled, he could start practicing his "pretty please."

The cabbie turned around and glared at him. "Hey, buddy!"

"Well, Zara?" he pressed. "What'll it be? We gonna settle this or not?"

She closed her eyes briefly and took a deep breath; he felt her chest move beneath him. "You're going to believe what you want to believe. And I'm exhausted from trying to talk sense into you."

"Well, now, that's progress, but it isn't exactly full disclosure. I guess I need to hear it from your own lips that you're really Zara Sutcliffe."

She rolled her eyes. "I'm really Zara Sutcliffe. Happy?"

"Happier." He smiled. "Leastways, now you're being honest with me. Only thing in the world I truly can't stomach is being lied to." Pushing away from her, he extracted a ten from his wallet and handed it to the mollified driver, then escorted Zara out of the cab and into the Plaza Hotel.

4

"I'M SORRY, Dr. Foster," the desk clerk said, "but there are no rooms with two double beds available."

Emma saw the clerk, a youngish man who bore a disconcerting resemblance to the Pillsbury Doughboy, give her a quick once-over, his studiously blank gaze taking in her torn stockings, harlot yellow suit, tangled hair. She had to admit she looked just a tad out of place surrounded by all this deeply polished, old-money opulence. Her self-consciousness was magnified by the lack of her big, familiar bag with its comforting inventory of essentials; she felt naked without it.

Gage rested his hands on his blue-jeaned hips. "When I checked in earlier this afternoon, I was told I had my pick of a king or two doubles."

"That was this afternoon." The Doughboy responded with the kind of studied politeness that implied some level of mental incapacitation on the part of the person being spoken to. "It's—" he glanced at his pretend Rolex "—almost six-thirty now, and we're booked up. All our rooms are taken. There are no more rooms with two beds left."

Gage rubbed his jaw and looked in Emma's direction. Now she was supposed to reassure him that it was okay, that one king-size bed for the two of them would do just fine. Instead she asked the clerk, "Do you have any cots?"

The Doughboy shook his head. "We ran out of them an

hour ago." With an insolently knowing look in Gage's direction, he added, "I apologize for the inconvenience."

"That's all right," Gage replied, and indeed, he didn't seem troubled at all. Not at all.

"It's no big deal," he assured her as he led her away from the front desk and through the sumptuous lobby. "There's this couchlike thing up there. I'll be perfectly happy to sleep on that if you want."

If you want. Those three little words were charged with meaning, Emma reflected, as Gage ushered her into an elevator and punched a button. They implied a certain...latitude for negotiation, which did nothing to reassure her of Gage Foster's innocent intent.

Southern gentleman or no, she knew he found her—or rather, her all dressed up like Zara Sutcliffe—sexually attractive. She saw the way his gaze lingered on her sometimes, heard the hint of suggestion in things he said. But most of all, she felt it—a high, ambient buzz of awareness, like the barely discernible drone of electricity near high power lines. An intimate form of energy coursed between them, making her feel ultrasensitized and a little lightheaded whenever he was close to her—as he was now, in this too-small elevator. Closing her eyes, she leaned back against the wall as they ascended.

"Zara?" She felt Gage's hand on her shoulder. "You all right?"

Zara. Her head began to pulse just above her right eye. Maybe Muldoon was right, and she *was* hurt worse than she'd thought. More likely it was just a tension headache, a reaction to the irony of having to pretend to be someone else in order to mollify a man whose hot button appeared to be dishonesty.

He gripped both shoulders now; she felt the warmth of his breath on her face. "You all right, Zara?"

She opened her eyes to find him leaning down close to her, his gaze slightly anxious.

"I'm fine," she assured him. "Fine. Just a little tired."

"You can lie down in the room."

When the doors opened, he surprised her by taking her hand to lead her down the hall to his room. Unlocking the door, he opened it and gestured her in ahead of him and flicked on the light switch.

"Wow." It was the most luxurious hotel room she'd ever been in: velvet drapes, oriental rugs and an embroidered coverlet on the colossal four-poster. In one corner stood a freestanding cheval mirror with etched glass. At an angle nearby was a chaise longue—the "couchlike thing," Emma assumed—upholstered in cream-on-cream striped silk, with a flowered throw and a couple of needlepoint pillows tossed artfully across it. "It's like I've died and gone to Martha Stewart's."

"It's a bit much for my taste."

Emma imagined that was true, remembering the handsomely rustic log house in the picture on the jacket of *Incision*. Gage lifted a worn leather duffel bag from the bed and tossed it into a corner. "You can lie down if you want." He helped her off with her coat and then hung it, complete with ray gun, in the closet.

"As long as I can get out of these—" Emma kicked off the stiletto-heeled pumps "—I'll be fine." She sat on a Queen Anne chair next to a gleaming mahogany table. A parchment-shaded lamp cast a buttery corona of light on an arrangement of white lilacs in a crystal vase, a room-service menu and a beige telephone. She breathed in a faint and pleasing perfume: lilacs and lemon oil. "This must be costing you a bundle."

"Costing *you* a bundle, don't you mean?"

"Excuse me?"

"Don't be gettin' cheap on me, sweetheart."

"I don't know what you're—"

"You don't remember pleading with me to come to New York—at your expense? 'I'll put you up at the Plaza and introduce you to some editors. We'll do the Russian Tea Room.' I don't even like tea. And I sure as shootin' don't have any use for subways and maniac purse snatchers and pissant little desk clerks, not to mention traffic and noise and filth and funky odors you don't know *where* they came from. And talk about overpopulation." He shook his head. "There's just *way* the hell too many people breathin' my air." He frowned. "Damn, I swore in front of you again."

She chuckled tiredly. "You're not crazy about New York, are you? Don't hold back—you can be frank with me."

"This town sucks like a tubful of ticks. You're a bright girl," he added wryly. "Surely you've noticed."

"Have I ever. I can't stand New York."

"Then why do you work here?"

"I have no choice."

She was about to blurt out her tale of woe—losing her freelance work and being forced to move here and take the dreaded staff job at *Crafty Lady*—unmindful of the fact that it was Emma's tale and not Zara's, when he said, "Yeah, I guess if you want to play the hotshot literary agent, you're pretty much stuck with New York."

"Guess so." Emma sighed, picking up the phone.

"Who are you calling?"

"I was supposed to meet…this guy, at his office this afternoon, but of course, I never showed—"

"Seems to be a bad habit of yours," Gage muttered as he unzipped his duffel and dumped its contents into a bureau drawer, except for a leather toilet kit, which he took to the bathroom.

Glaring at his back, Emma called information for Mac-

Gowan Byrne's number in SoHo, dialed it and got an answering machine. A woman's crisp voice said, "You have reached the office of MacGowan Byrne Ltd. Leave a message and your call will be returned as soon as possible."

Beep.

"Mr. Byrne," Emma said, "this is, um...Zara Sutcliffe."

Gage smirked at her as he exited the bathroom; she raised her chin and turned haughtily away.

She said, "I'm sorry I had to miss our meeting this afternoon. Actually, I guess it'll be tomorrow by the time you listen to this, so the meeting would have been yesterday afternoon. Circumstances...well...anyway, I'm sorry. I still very much want to conclude this transaction. Please call me at my home number, 718-555-5734. That's in—"

Beep.

"Queens." Emma replaced the receiver in its cradle.

"Queens?" Gage took off his jacket and hung it up. "I thought only administrative assistants lived in Queens. I woulda pictured Zara Sutcliffe...I don't know. In some swanky apartment on the Upper East Side. Something with lots of glass and marble and...columns. Big ol' important-looking columns."

Bingo. He'd just described Zara's home to a *T*. "Shows what you know," she bluffed. "So happens Flushing, Queens, is a very happening place right now. Very trendy. Everyone's moving there."

He squinted at her, hands on hips. "Flushing? Where Shea Stadium is? I've been there. Isn't there a fat-rendering plant there that stinks to high heaven? Flushing River doesn't smell too good, either, now that I think about it. Hungry?"

"Not anymore."

Gage took the receiver, but waved away the room-service menu. "Yeah, this is Gage Foster up in 602.

Can y'all make me up a couple of burgers, well done, with plenty of fried onions? Good. Now, when I say well done, I mean *cooked*. Don't just hurt it, kill it dead." He paused. "*No*, I don't want any pink inside. No! None! Cooked. Through and through. Gray on the inside, black on the outside. Black. You writin' this down? Well, write it down. Get a pen, I'll wait." He waited. "Black. *B-L-A-C-K*. On the outside. *G-R-A-Y* on the inside. Cooked. You got that? All right, and some fries and whatnot. Also a bottle of Jack Daniels and two glasses. That's it, thanks." He pressed the switch hook.

"Maybe I like my burgers rare."

"So does *E. coli*." He dialed another number before she could take the receiver back from him. "Is this the concierge? Yeah, this is Gage Foster in 602. Can I get some first-aid supplies sent up to the room? Some hydrogen peroxide, some gauze pads and tape, and maybe a tube of antibiotic ointment. Stat. I mean, thanks." He hit the switch hook and gave Emma the phone. "Gotta do something about those knees of yours."

"They're not that bad."

"Even so, they should be cleaned and bandaged."

The first-aid stuff was delivered in record time.

"Let's do this in here," Gage said, motioning for her to follow him into the brightly lit, white-tiled bathroom. He shoved aside his toilet kit and the various hotel-supplied toiletries and glasses laid out on the vanity, then unfolded a clean towel and set the first-aid supplies on top of it. Unbuttoning the cuffs of his blue chambray shirt, he rolled up the sleeves, then unwrapped a bar of soap, turned on the tap and scrubbed his hands. He really worked at them, washing them with the germ-conscious zeal of a surgeon, which, of course, he was—or, as he'd hastened to point out, *used to be.* Steam rose from the basin and she knew the water must be scalding.

Emma noticed something then, something about his right hand that she hadn't seen before, because she hadn't really looked at it. The little finger on that hand was truncated about halfway up; the tip of the ring finger was missing as well. In addition, several savage-looking scars marred his hand and wrist. From the slightly awkward way he held it, she could tell he didn't have full use of it.

Gage noticed the direction of her gaze as he was rinsing his hands. "Don't worry, I can still handle gauze and adhesive tape. Just can't cut a straight line with a scalpel."

"That's why you're not a surgeon anymore?"

He whipped another hand towel off the rack. "That's right."

She hesitated. "What happened?"

He nodded toward her legs. "You want to get those stockings off?"

"Oh. Yeah." Turning her back to him, Emma leaned over, lifted the hem of the yellow leather skirt and studied the baffling little clasps that connected the stockings to the garter belt.

From behind her he sighed. "I got knifed by a crack-head at St. Vincent Infirmary in Little Rock. He went for my throat, and like the jackass I am, I shielded it with my hand."

She turned around in time to see him wad the damp towel into a ball and hurl it into the corner. "And that," he said, "was the end of my career as a general surgeon."

"I'm sorry." Returning her attention to the stockings, she started fiddling with one of the clasps, wishing she'd paid more attention when her mother had attached it. She prodded it, yanked on it...she even tried to tear the stocking, all to no avail.

Gage came to stand in front of her. "Need some help?"

"No." Emma let go of the skirt and backed up until she felt the vanity behind her.

"Don't be shy." He dropped to one knee and reached up under her skirt with both hands. "I'm a doctor."

"I—I thought you were an ex-doctor," she stammered, as he felt around on her right thigh for the connection. His hands were hot from being washed, his fingertips slightly rough. When they brushed her bare thigh above the stocking, she had to bite her lip to keep from gasping.

"Maybe," he said with a devilish smile as he deftly flicked the little clip open, "but I still haven't forgotten how to play doctor." He reached around to the back—Emma held her breath—and undid that one just as easily.

She licked her dry lips and strove for a nonchalant tone. "You're good at that."

"I've probably had more practice at it than you have." He glided the stocking slowly downward, gathering it up as it went, igniting a shivery path of sensation. "Is this the first time you've worn these?"

"Yes." But it obviously wasn't the first time he'd removed them from a woman. Emma wondered about his past. According to the *Incision* bio, he was thirty-nine and had never been married; he lived all by himself in that big log house in the middle of an Arkansas pine forest, with only his dogs and horses for company. But a man like Gage Foster—part cowboy, part doctor, part bestselling author—could hardly lack for female companionship.

He paused at the knee, carefully peeling the ripped and bloodied silk stocking away from the raw flesh there. "Does this hurt?"

"A little."

He looked up at her, his eyes stunningly blue in the shiny white bathroom. "I'll be careful. I'll try not to hurt you."

She swallowed. "Thanks."

He retrieved his reading glasses from his shirt pocket with one hand, flipped them open and settled them on his face. Peering closely at her knee, he stripped the stocking away from the wound with an exceedingly gentle touch, his brow furrowed in concentration. His large hands were precise in their movements, even the bad one, of which he could only effectively use three fingers; the long muscles of his forearms shifted as he worked.

"There you go." He slid the stocking off her leg and tossed it in the trash.

"Do you miss being a surgeon?"

His jaw clenched. "To say I miss it would be a grave understatement." Snaking his hands swiftly under her skirt again—*flick, flick*—he lowered the other stocking, once more taking great pains over her knee. The second stocking joined the first in the trash, and then he laid a folded bath towel on the lid of the toilet and invited her to sit.

She did, tugging on her skirt in a vain attempt to keep it from riding up quite so high; she felt half-naked, even though it was just her legs that were exposed. He tucked the bath mat under her bare feet so she wouldn't have to rest them on the cold tiled floor, which struck her as an exceptionally thoughtful gesture.

Compelled to find out more about him despite his ambivalence, she said, "If you liked practicing medicine so much, how come you didn't just change your specialty to something that didn't require such great manual dexterity?"

"It wasn't medicine I liked, it was surgery." He washed his hands again; she could almost see him in his scrubs and mask, getting ready to operate. "I'm not sure I've got the people skills it would take to be a really good physician—I mean, someone who has to actually talk to patients and relate to them."

Emma could well believe that, given his opinion of the human race as inherently lacking in integrity. "What about teaching? Did you think about that?"

"Of course. Three different medical schools offered me professorships, and I considered it, but again, dealing with all those students...I just couldn't see it. And after what I'd been through in med school..." He shook his head grimly, then soaped up a washcloth. "I'm gonna start by cleaning those knees. You've got some grit from the track embedded in there."

"What about med school?" she persisted as he squatted down and began gently stroking her right knee with the washcloth.

"Does that sting?"

"No," she lied. "What about med school?"

"What about it?"

"You were going to tell me what you'd been through in med school."

"No I wasn't." He rinsed the knee he'd cleaned and moved to the other one. "I just mentioned it, is all."

"Tease."

He glanced up at her, smiling crookedly. "Sweetheart, when I tease you, you'll know it." He bent his head to his work again; she leaned over to watch him as he painstakingly dislodged the little bits of dirt that had gotten ground into her knee.

He smelled good. His natural smell—she could tell it hadn't come out of a bottle—was the smell they tried to recreate when they made men's colognes, clean and woodsy and masculine. She leaned closer. And warm, and just a tiny bit spicy.

"Med school," he said without looking up, "was when it

truly started to dawn on me that most folks are basically unscrupulous and self-serving. It was a real eye-opener for me the first time a professor I was assisting took my research and published it as his own. Everyone I told about it just shrugged."

"I've heard about that kind of thing," Emma said. She'd read about it, too, recently. When was that?

"It happened again, with another professor, guy named Snyder," Gage said, as he picked up a towel and patted both knees dry. "Except he actually took a paper I'd written and put his name on it. I blew him in—reported the plagiarism to the administration—but they treated me like a pariah for my disloyalty. Let him off with a warning. I asked around, and I wasn't the only one this had happened to—not just with Snyder, but with others."

"That's terrible."

Gage soaked a gauze pad with peroxide and dabbed the wound on her right knee, producing a ticklish foam. "Dr. Snyder's still a very respected figure at that school. And for all I know, he's still ripping off his students' work, calling it his own."

"Why? I mean, why doesn't he just..." She shrugged.

"Write his *own* papers? That takes time, effort and a clear mind, unmuddled by the various and sundry tranquilizers and barbiturates he used to scam out of the pharmacy."

"He took drugs?" Emma asked, the pieces falling into place.

Gage moved to her left knee. "Drug use was an epidemic at that school, by both the teaching staff and the students. Amphetamines were the most popular. All kinds of narcotics were being used."

"You wrote about all this in *Incision*," she said. "Only you changed the names."

"And the circumstances," he said, "just enough so I couldn't get slapped with any lawsuits."

"It's all in there, though. That scene in the first chapter, where Dr. Whoozits, the bad guy—"

Gage laughed as he tore the paper from another gauze pad. "'Dr. Whoozits, the bad guy'? So much for in-depth characterization."

"The one who ends up killing all those people. He shoots up right before he goes into the operating room. And then, in chapter two, he's accused of plagiarism—"

"Yeah, only Snyder never committed murder...that I know of." Gage squeezed antibiotic ointment onto the gauze pad and pressed it gently over her right knee.

Closing her eyes, she murmured, "Mmm, that feels good." When she opened them, she found him looking at her, his smile belying the intensity of his gaze.

"I aim to please." He taped the pad down, then prepared another one.

The silence felt too close, too charged, especially with him kneeling in front of her, ministering to her this way. "So," Emma said, "you tapped your med-school experiences when you set out to write *Incision?*"

"Actually, I wrote it during med school. Or rather, started it then." He smoothed the second pad down and tore off some tape. "It was my way of dealing with things, the frustration of being surrounded by all this corruption and having no way to fight it. Once I started my practice, I set it aside—I just didn't have the time to work on it. It sat under my bed for thirteen years."

"What prompted you to finish it?"

Gage shrugged his wide shoulders as he pressed the tape into place. "Got my hand cut up and couldn't operate. I was at home, recuperating, and the book seemed like a good way to kill time while I tried to figure out what to do with the rest of my life. When it was done, I stuck it back under the bed."

"You're kidding."

"If Gracie hadn't found it, it'd still be—"

"Gracie?" Absurd disappointment burned in Emma's stomach. Ah. So there was a Gracie.

"Picture a Mack truck in a housedress."

"All right...." Not quite what she would have envisioned as Gage Foster's type.

"My housekeeper." Rising slowly, he removed his glasses and tucked them back in his shirt pocket.

Emma smiled. "Ah."

He recapped the antibiotic tube and the bottle of peroxide. "Anyway, I walked into my room one day and found her propped up on the bed with a dust mop next to her and my manuscript on her lap—she looked to be about halfway through it. She started hollerin' at me—how come I kept it hidden away like I did? I should send it to one of those big New York publishers. Finally I did, just to shut her up and get her back to cleaning. I expected to get one of those form rejection notes and wave it under her nose and maybe then she'd leave me alone."

"Instead," Emma said, "you got a record advance for a first novel. At least, that's what I heard."

"You heard right." He leaned against the vanity and crossed his arms, shaking his head. "Which only goes to show where people's priorities are. It would have taken me years of practicing surgery to make what I did on that one advance."

"So?"

"So I just think the world's a pretty screwed-up place if I get rewarded better for makin' up an idiotic tale about evil Dr. Whoozits than for savin' people's lives."

"Oh, I don't know about that. I don't think—"

A knock came at the door. "Room service."

Gage held out his hand to help Emma to her feet. "You can finish telling me how wrongheaded I am while we eat."

As soon as the room-service guy left—after setting their burgers and fries and coleslaw out on a little linen-covered table, as if it were haute cuisine—Gage opened the bottle of Jack Daniels, poured some into a glass and handed it to her. "A little Dr. Daniels's Ladies Tonic—for medicinal purposes, of course."

"Uh..."

"Think of it as liquid Valium. You've had a rough day." He poured himself a little, then sat at the table, motioning for her to sit opposite him, which she did.

Emma sniffed the amber liquid and winced. She couldn't stand the taste of alcohol; once a year, she tried a sip of wine at Thanksgiving dinner, and that was always enough to keep her away from the stuff. Of course, he would assume Zara Sutcliffe drank; it was part of your job description if you were the Life of the Party.

"You don't have to drink it," he said, eyeing her curiously. "I'm not trying to force it on you, I just thought maybe it would relax you."

Relax her? That might not be such a bad idea, given the state of her nerves, and the fact that she still had to spend the *night* with this man, in the very same *room*. Raising the glass to her mouth, she closed her eyes, held her breath and took a generous gulp.

"There you go." He lifted the lid from a small silver bowl. "Coleslaw?"

Emma's eyes burned with tears of shock; her nostrils flared, her throat convulsed. She nodded spastically as she strained to force the contents of her mouth into her throat.

"Fries?"

More frantic nodding as she swallowed, the whiskey

scouring a red-hot trail all the way into her stomach. She
sucked in a breath, which snagged in her throat, precipitat-
ing a coughing fit.

Gage paused in the act of scooping French fries onto his
plate. "You all right?"

She nodded again as she continued coughing.

"You swallow the wrong way?" He rose and circled the
little table.

Nod nod nod, cough cough cough. She was in hell. This was
hell. The train did get her, she'd died, and now she was going to have to spend eternity with Gage Foster, suffering
one humiliation after another as she pretended to be Zara.

He squatted down next to her, one big hand rubbing her
back in circles, the other resting on her thigh. Her bare
thigh. "Just relax," he gently urged.

Oh, yeah.

"Take slow breaths. That's right."

Gradually the coughing subsided. "I'm okay," she
croaked. "Thank you."

"Here." Gaining his feet, he poured some ice water from
a pitcher into a glass and handed it to her. "Drink this."

She did. "That's better. Thanks."

He sat down and took a big bite out of his hamburger, inspecting it closely as he chewed. Apparently satisfied with
its level of grayness, he said, "It looks fine."

She lifted the top half of the bun and inspected the
charred lump of meat. "It looks burned."

"It's just done." He picked up some fries with his fingers
and shoved them into his mouth.

"It's cremated. And you're wrong about your book. It is
not idiotic."

He swallowed another bite of burger. "I was hoping
you'd decided to drop that line of conversation."

"Why?" She speared a French fry with her fork. "You

don't like people telling you what a brilliant writer you are?"

"I was a brilliant surgeon. What I am now is a guy gettin' paid obscene amounts of money for makin' stuff up as he goes along. There are Americans living on the streets. I just read that forty-eight percent of the chronically poor in the U.S. are children, and they're paying a hack writer that kind of whipout? It isn't right."

"If the money bothers you so much," she said, gesturing with her fork as he chowed down on his burger, "give it to charity."

"I do," he said. "Most of it, anyway."

"Oh." To cover her surprise, she lifted her glass and drained it before registering that it was the Jack Daniels, not the water. Her eyes bugged out as the whiskey went down, but through an effort of will she kept from choking; or maybe her throat was still in a state of shock from its previous dose of Ladies Tonic. "That's very generous of you," she rasped.

"It's not just the money," he said, tilting the bottle over her glass automatically, like an attentive host at a dinner party. "It's the whole idea of writing pulp fiction for a living. That's a heck of a way for a grown man to earn his keep, if you ask me. I mean, any clown with a word processor can sit down and bang out a potboiler."

"That's ridiculous. Telling a good story takes talent and hard work and...and heart. No one can just sit down and write one, I don't care what you say—not a story like *Incision*, anyway. I remember I went to bed with it, thinking I'd read the first couple of chapters before I fell asleep, but it kept me awake all night."

"Yeah?" A hot spark lit his eyes for just a moment; a slow, masculine smile pulled at one corner of his mouth.

She reached for her glass automatically. This time she noticed it was the whiskey before she put it to her mouth, but she steeled herself and drank it down anyway. *Why not, if it'll relax me? I could use a little calming down right about now.*

"If I could write like you do," she said, dragging the whiskey bottle toward her, "I wouldn't be doing what I'm doing, I can damn well assure you of that." Whoa! She never cursed. Yet she just had. And it felt great. "Dammit," she added resolutely as she poured.

"Uh..." Gage wrapped his hand around the bottle and gently extracted it from her grip, setting it next to him, out of her reach. "Maybe you'd better have a little more to eat before you and Dr. Daniels get too chummy there. I'm not fixin' to get you hammered. I just meant to help you unwind a little."

"I won't get drunk." She waved a hand airily, and it seemed to move in slow motion; she'd never felt so graceful. "I've never been drunk in my life." Leaning forward, she wagged a finger at him to emphasize the point. "Not once."

"Let's just keep it that way. Why don't you eat some of that burger? It's really very good."

"Will it make you happy?" she asked winsomely. Another hurdle leapt; she'd never been winsome before.

"Exceedingly."

"Well, then." She lifted the burger, took a bite, chewed. He watched her the whole time. She discovered that she loved being watched. "It *is* good!" she exclaimed in genuine delight. "That charcoal crust around the meat? It really adds something." She tossed back the rest of her whiskey; he frowned. "Don't worry. I told you. Never drunk a day in my life."

After she'd polished off the burger—it really was extraordinarily good; she'd never *imagined* a hamburger could taste like that—he said, "So you want to write novels."

She paused in the act of oh-so-delicately dabbing her mouth with her linen napkin. "Did I say that?"

"Not in so many words, but it's obvious from some of the things you said, and your whole attitude toward writing."

Silently marveling at his perception, she said, "I think about it sometimes. Sometimes I think...no, you'll think it's stupid."

"No I won't." He leaned forward on his elbows, his gaze riveted on her. "I want to hear about it."

"I've never told anyone."

His voice grew softer, deeper. "Tell *me*."

She bit her lip. His eyes zeroed in on her mouth. His throat moved as he swallowed.

Emma saw herself from his perspective, a flushed young woman, inky hair askew, eyes glittering from just a bit too much Dr. Daniels, biting her lip....

She felt beautiful...desirable. She'd never felt desirable before, never felt the heat of a man's gaze, the hunger, the wanting....

She liked it. It thrilled her, speeded her heart, made her shiver with anticipation.

Yes. Anticipation. She knew what Gage Foster saw as he looked at her, and she knew what he wanted. And, to her astonishment, she wanted it, too. For the first time in her life, she finally wanted—really wanted—what she'd denied herself for way too long. In less than a month she'd be thirty years old. Did she really want to be a virgin when she blew out thirty candles?

Omigod, I think I might actually do this.

"Zara," he said in a soft rumble that vibrated right through her. "Tell me."

Zara. Zara, tell me.

It was Zara he wanted, Zara he desired. Of course.

She was wearing Zara's clothes, not to mention her man-killer rep. Zara, queen of the broken hearts. Of course he wanted her. Everyone wanted Zara.

"Tell me," he repeated. "You want to write novels?"

Emma nodded.

"What kind? Glitzy romance, right?"

She shook her head.

"A roman à clef about the publishing industry?"

She shook her head again. "Mysteries. Whodunits."

His eyebrows rose. "Whodunits."

"Cozy ones."

"*Cozies?*" he laughed.

"What's so funny?"

"Nothing, I just...it's just that I wouldn't have imagined Zara Sutcliffe writing about little-old-lady sleuths, is all."

"Well, imagine it," she said testily.

"Look, don't take offense," he said. "Actually, I think it's really cool."

"Uh-huh."

"Can I let you in on a little secret?"

"Shoot."

"I watched every episode of *Murder, She Wrote*."

"You did?"

"Every frickin' frackin' one—" he held up his hand "—as God is my witness."

"Me, too," she confessed in a winsome whisper, loving her winsomeness, loving this conversation, loving...*liking* him. A lot. Despite the fact that he thought she was Zara. That wasn't really his fault. Well, it was, kind of. Actually, very much so, seeing as he stubbornly refused to let her correct the mistaken identity, but she could overlook that because of extenuating circumstances—to wit, his really very admirable character.

An inventory of Gage Foster's admirable character traits scrolled through her mind:

1. He was ruggedly good-looking. That one just popped up first; it didn't mean she was shallow.
2. He was honest and honorable. To a fault, probably, but can there really be too much of a good thing?
3. He was brave; he'd jumped down on those subway tracks to save her.
4. He was a doctor. Or ex-doctor, depending on what mood he was in.
5. He was The Next Grisham, for crying out loud.
6. He liked *Murder, She Wrote*.
7. He was sexy as hell.

Emma had never really—*really*—thought of a man as sexy. Until now. But, boy, was he. Ever.

"So," he asked, "have you written any cozy whodunits yet?"

She struggled to redirect her train of thought to the subject at hand. "It's hard to find the time." A lame excuse, now that she heard it coming out of her mouth; she should have written one while she was freelancing, because if she couldn't find the time then, she sure wouldn't find it now.

"You live a hectic, high-powered life," he said, "but if it's important to you, you've gotta find time." Leaning across the table, he took her hand and squeezed, looking at her with those neon blue eyes that seemed to drill right into her soul. "If there's something you really want, sometimes you just have to go for it."

The image of a birthday cake ablaze with thirty candles materialized in Emma's mind's eye.

"You think?" she asked softly.

"Absolutely." He squeezed her hand again; actually, it was more of a caress, a slow massage with those big, slightly rough fingers of his. "Life's too short to wait around for it to happen to you. Sometimes you just have to go ahead and make it happen."

The breath seemed to have gotten sucked from her lungs; all she could do was nod.

He rose and gathered the remains of their dinner on the big room-service tray, all except the bottle of Jack Daniels and the two glasses, which he left on the table. While he was taking the tray out to the hall, Emma quickly poured herself a fortifying shot of whiskey and drank it, relishing the heat that slid down her throat and bloomed in her stomach. It felt like courage—false courage, to be sure, but right now she'd take anything she could get.

She was going to do this. *Omigod*, she was really going to do this.

MACGOWAN BYRNE, sitting with his feet propped on a lacquer-and-ormolu desk that had once belonged to Czar Nicholas II—but then everything in Russia had once belonged to him, lucky bastard—took another gulp from his bottle of Absolut, punched the Play button on the answering machine and listened to it again:

"Mr. Byrne, this is, um...Zara Sutcliffe...."

Right. Mac plucked the driver's license out of the tacky, pink vinyl wallet on his lap and held it under his Tiffany lamp for the fiftieth time since acquiring it, along with the rest of that grotesque pile of crap in the middle of his desk. He squinted at it through a haze of slowly escalating wrath, seeing Zara Sutcliffe's face, but reading Emma Sutcliffe's name.

"I'm sorry I had to miss our meeting this afternoon," asserted the soft, smoothly credible voice of the lying bitch who had the nerve to try and scam him; correction, one of the *two* lying bitches who had the nerve to try and scam him, because Zara was in on it, of course. Zara had no doubt masterminded this little masquerade. When *would* he learn to stop trusting people?

"Actually," the voice continued, "I guess it'll be tomorrow by the time you listen to this, so the meeting would have been yesterday afternoon." Wrong. He'd monitored the call when it came in, having been right here in his office all evening, sorting through the effluvia of her pathetic life—the only remotely useful item in that bag being the can of pepper spray, which she should have used on him and didn't, foolish girl—searching vainly for clues as to what the devil these two lying, scheming bitches were trying to do to him.

"Circumstances...well..." Yeah, Mac knew all about the circumstances. He'd engineered them personally, in full costume and makeup, for all the good it did him. He'd intended it to be so swift, so simple: wait outside her office building when she left for their meeting, lure her into a secluded doorway, open her throat—he lifted his exquisite Indo-Persian dagger from his desk and ran his thumb along its razor edge—snatch the ray gun and dissolve into the crowd, another invisible bum in a city teeming with them. No one knew about the ray gun deal—or so he'd thought, but you really couldn't trust anyone anymore—so with Zara Sutcliffe on ice and the gun in his possession, he'd be beyond suspicion and two million dollars richer.

A slick plan, only it hadn't turned out quite so swift or simple after rush-hour gridlock forced his quarry underground. He'd had to substitute a subway train for his exquisite dagger, which would have been fine and good—better, probably—if it hadn't been for the clown in the cowboy boots who just had to play hero. And if the ray gun had been in the bitch's handbag, which it wasn't.

Why not, if she'd been on her way to sell it to him? Just

exactly what little intrigue had the Sisters Sutcliffe cooked up to sucker him out of his—*his*—two million? They probably thought he was just a harmlessly legitimate dealer in collectibles, a patsy they could dupe out of the money *and* the ray gun.

Mac smiled grimly as he brought the bottle to his mouth again. They really had no idea. No idea at all, the things he was capable of...the things he'd done...the things he had yet to do...to them.

"I still very much want to conclude this transaction." *You and me both, honey; oh, yeah, I definitely feel the need for some sort of closure on this.* "Please call me at my home number, 718-555-5734. That's in—"

Beep.

Queens, for God's sake. Flushing, Queens, of all putrescent stinkholes, which was why he was sucking down vodka the way he was, to get in the proper frame of mind to cross the lousy Fifty-ninth Street Bridge into Archie Bunkerland tonight.

Because he had to do it. He had to find that ray gun—that was his first priority. If it wasn't at Emma's place, he'd check Zara's, and if it wasn't there...well, then he might have to get Indo-Persian on their asses.

The phone rang. Mac took another hit of vodka and let the machine kick in. "You have reached the office of MacGowan Byrne Ltd...."

"Pick up, Mac. It's William."

Damn. Mac thunked the bottle on the desk, lifted the receiver and turned off the machine. "It's almost nine o'clock, William. Isn't that past your bedtime?"

"Do you have the ray gun?" The old guy always got right to the point.

Mac held the dagger by its bone handle and turned it slowly, admiring the way the watered-steel blade shimmered in the amber glow of the Tiffany lamp. "I'm working on it."

There was a second of dead air. "You said you'd have it for me tonight."

"Things have gotten...complicated."

"I'm going to pay two million dollars for that ray gun. You said you could come up with it. That sounded pretty simple to me."

"To me, too, till the daughter decided to haggle me into the ground." Avaricious bitch. Mac had figured she'd want to up the price; he'd been ready to go up into six figures. But Zara Sutcliffe was a real pit bull when it came to negotiating, grabbing on and not letting go till she'd squeezed every last dollar out of him. Two million of them, to be precise. Which resulted in a profit for Mac of exactly zero percent—if he was idiot enough to pay her, which he wasn't. Her greed had forced him to his present course of action, namely stealing what had proved too costly to purchase and eliminating everyone who could point the finger at him. It wasn't the first time he'd gone this route to obtain a prized collectible, but it was the first time things had gotten quite so out of his control.

"Why shouldn't she negotiate?" William asked. "From what I hear, Zara Sutcliffe's a smart cookie. Good for her if she got your commission down—more money for her mother."

"She robbed me," Mac growled.

William chuckled. "She got the upper hand. You're probably not used to that. Now you know how it feels. But, hey. Whatever deal you struck for that thing, that's between you and the Sutcliffes. If you screwed up somehow, that's none of my concern.

"All I really care about," William was saying, "is that I

offered you two million dollars for Candy Carmelle's ray gun, and I want it. Now."

"What is this thing you've got for her?" Mac mused aloud as he scraped the dagger's blade along his jaw. Not for the first time, he wondered what on earth the old man had been thinking when he offered to pay *two million dollars* for that gun. Not that Mac didn't understand the obsessive-compulsive nature of collectors; no one understood those lunatics better. And William had the biggest collection of Candy Carmelle memorabilia—the only collection, probably—in existence. But *two million?* Maybe he was going senile; if so, Mac would have to milk his dementia for all it was worth. "Candy Carmelle...I mean, she's a hot ticket and all. Used to be, anyway, back when I was a kid and she was still acting. I was pretty hung up on her myself. But I grew up and got over it. Sounds to me like you're still nursing a crush on a starlet who's probably a withered-up old crone by now—"

"My interest in what I purchase is my business entirely, Byrne, and don't you forget it."

"Chill, William. I was just trying to make—"

"You were just trying to deflect this discussion from the subject at hand, which is the fact that you have failed to produce the item you promised."

Mac lowered his feet off the desk and sat up straight. "Wrong. I may have failed to produce it when I said I would. Circumstances..." Listen to him, whining his excuses like that twit Emma Sutcliffe. "I'll get it. No matter what it takes."

Another pause ensued, this one crackling with tension. "What's that supposed to mean?"

Mac grinned, suddenly enjoying this immensely. He slid open his top desk drawer and admired its contents: the brace of gleaming steel throwing knives in their leather sheath; the Japanese *yoroi-toshi* dagger with its thick, armor-piercing blade; and a small Indian crutch sword, its hilt damascened in gold and silver. All were good for dispatching problems silently, a boon in a city where privacy was at a premium. And, of course, there was his sleek little Smith & Wesson Sigma—not silent, nor particularly refined, but elegant in its efficiency. "My methods of acquisition are my business entirely," he said, parroting William's own words back at him, "and don't you forget it."

"You're starting to sound a little scorched around the edges, Byrne. I won't have you leaning on anyone. That was never part of the plan."

"The plan is mine," Mac reminded him, sheathing his dagger and returning it to the drawer. "The money is yours. I'll do what I have to do."

"Mac, don't do any—"

"Ciao, William. I'll call you when I've got the gun."

Mac slammed the phone in its cradle, stood up and began scooping Emma Sutcliffe's heap of junk into the big, quilted bag it had come out of; all evidence must be destroyed so that no one could ever trace this business back to him. It was a shame, really, because he rather liked the bag. It had a kind of rustic insouciance that might bring a pretty penny in Europe, where some of his clients had a weakness for naive Americana.

When the bag was once more bulging with its absurd load, Mac carried it out into the hall, opened the little metal door that led down into the incinerator and crammed it in. He listened to it slide down the chute, heard it land among the rest of the trash, and closed the door.

By tomorrow morning it would be a handful of ash. He wished the rest of it could be that easy.

5

EMMA CHEWED ON HER LIP as Gage reentered the room, locking the door behind him. "Well," he asked, "what's your pleasure?"

"What?"

"We've had dinner." He slowly approached the table where she sat, his long-legged stride graceful in a kind of loose-limbed-cowboy way. "You've gotten your boo-boos fixed." He grinned sheepishly. "I've talked about myself way the hell more—dammit, sorry—a lot more than a fella has any right to, but you encouraged it, so it's really your fault." He stopped directly in front of her and looked down; he wasn't grinning anymore, just regarding her with an attitude of quiet expectancy. "What do you want to do now?"

What would Zara say? How did you seduce someone? Well, maybe *seduce* wasn't the right word, given the seducee's obvious interest and enthusiasm.

How, then, did a woman who was willing let a man who was willing know how willing she was?

Zara would know; she'd have all of this down cold by now. Emma remembered that moment back at Zara's office when Gage wouldn't let her go, and she'd changed herself into her sister, just like that adopting the mannerisms, the attitude, the poise. It had been quite a transformation—instantaneous, but momentous in its own peculiar way.

Being Zara had endowed her with power, confidence,

cleverness. For once in her life, she'd been able to think on her feet—*This author got a million five for the movie rights*—concocting a plan of escape on the spur of the moment and seeing it through to victory. And all because she'd put herself in her sister's mile-high stilettoes.

Now, no one knew better than Emma that Zara Sutcliffe's dazzling, larger-than-life image didn't quite mesh with reality. In a way, Zara herself pretended to be Zara—this superconfident, superalluring goddess of publishing—because it worked for her. Zara herself was just a human being with a human being's foibles and vulnerabilities. *But*...she'd perfected the Zara Sutcliffe that the world saw, internalizing it to the point where it had become a dyed-in-the-wool part of her. She could negotiate a million-dollar contract in her sleep. And when it came to men, well...Emma couldn't imagine a situation her twin hadn't encountered.

So, how would Zara handle this particular situation?

She'd just let it happen, Emma realized. Gage wanted her; she wanted him. They both knew it. There was really nothing to do. Let him be the aggressor; he seemed comfortable with that role, more comfortable than she would be, certainly.

Not that she couldn't help things along. Just a little. Nothing too goofy, no batting of the eyelashes or dropping of handkerchiefs. What would Zara do?

"Ah..." Arching her back, Emma locked her fingers and stretched her arms high over her head. As her eyes closed, she could almost *feel* Gage's gaze caressing her. She could see the yellow leather straining over her breasts, sense his hands tighten involuntarily as he imagined touching her.

This isn't so hard, she thought, opening her eyes to find him looking exactly where she knew he'd be looking.

She ran her fingers through her hair, enjoying this immensely. "What do I want to do now?" she mused as their gazes met. "I wouldn't mind combing my hair." She plucked at a tangle. "It's a mess."

"Oh." He nodded, looking just slightly shell-shocked. This really was fun. "Okay."

"Do you have a comb I can borrow?"

"Oh. Sure."

He went into the bathroom and unzipped his toilet kit. Emma quickly poured herself another dose of liquid fortitude. It was going down easier and easier. She could feel its warmth coursing through her. A sense of well-being enveloped her, along with a certain exhilarating fearlessness. Granted, things were just the tiniest bit swimmy around the edges—just the tiniest bit—but she could handle that.

She stood up, and the room surprised her by tilting to the side just for a second before righting itself.

Okay. So she was just a little bit tipsy. It wasn't too bad. She wasn't *drunk*—not really; she wasn't slurring her speech or anything.

Turning, she knocked over the chair she'd been sitting on, and was hurriedly setting it upright—at considerable expense to her equilibrium—when Gage walked back into the room.

"You all right?" he asked.

"Sure. I'm fine." She spoke slowly, enunciating every word carefully. "Is that the comb?" He handed her a small black Ace, a man's comb. "Thank you."

Her gaze lit on the chaise longue, set upright in front of the cheval mirror: perfect. She crossed to it and sat in the middle facing her reflection. Behind her, in the mirror, she saw him watching her intently as she began tugging the comb through her hair.

It snagged. She worked through the tangle and combed some more. It snagged again. Emma made a wry face, as if the strain of grooming herself was just too monumental, and met his gaze in the mirror. "Are you any good at combing hair?" she asked, holding up the comb.

He walked toward her until he stood directly behind her. His hand moved as if to reach for the comb, but then he withdrew it and folded his arms.

"Uh, listen," he said hesitantly. "I think there's something we should get clear between us. Now, before...well, now. I tried to tell you in the cab earlier, but we got sidetracked. I mean, I just don't want you harboring any misconceptions."

He look at her again in the mirror, and he must have seen the confusion on her face, because he said, "Ah, shoot," and shook his head in evident frustration. "Look, no offense or anything, but I really don't want you...I mean, I'm not interested in you..."

Emma's cheeks stung. She bolted to her feet, facing away from him across the chaise longue. "I think I understand." Boy, did she ever. *Idiot! Idiot! How could you make such a fool out of yourself?*

"I'm sure you're very good at it," he added hastily. "God knows you're experienced enough."

Experienced? Emma whirled to face him, felt her blood pressure escalating on her sister's behalf. "What, exactly, is that supposed to mean?"

He looked a little taken aback. "Well, I assumed...I mean, given your reputation and all—"

"Reputation?" Emma seethed with righteous indignation; it boiled within her, fueled by the unaccustomed heat of the alcohol flowing through her veins.

"I mean, you've been an agent for a long time," he said, "and you represent some of the hottest writers in the business. You must know what you're doing. I'm sure you're a wonderful agent, it's just that I don't think we're suited to each other—not in terms of an agent-client relationship, anyway."

"Oh." Emma sat back down, weak with relief. He wasn't rejecting her as a woman, he was rejecting her—or rather, her sister—as an agent. That was an altogether different and less mortifying prospect.

After a moment, he sat behind her on the chaise; in the mirror she saw him rubbing his jaw, his expression troubled. "Try and understand," he said, patting her shoulder consolingly, "it's just business."

"I know. It's okay."

"You're a terrific person, a very attrac— Huh? It's okay?"

"Of course it's okay," she said over her shoulder. "You don't want me for an agent." She shrugged. "You win some, you lose some."

He studied her as if trying to figure her out. "You're taking this with a great deal of grace."

She pushed the winsome lever up to full throttle. "I'm a very graceful person, in case you hadn't noticed."

He smoothed his hand from her shoulder down her arm, slowly. "Oh, there's not a lot about you that's managed to escape my notice." When his hand reached hers, he plucked the comb out of her fingers. "I never answered your question."

"What question?"

"Whether I'm any good at combing hair. As it happens, it's one of my few real talents."

"Is it?"

"It is indeed. Care for a demonstration?" He leaned closer, his body pressing against her from behind, the air between them alive with possibilities. "Pretty please?"

Pretty please? She managed to nod. "Yes, that would be…" Her voice caught; she cleared her throat. "Yes."

Is this foreplay? Emma wondered as Gage drew the comb

through her hair, pausing occasionally to work a knot loose and then slide his fingers through the newly smooth strands. It felt good—better than good, she thought, letting her eyes drift shut. It felt...hypnotically luxurious. The gentle tugging of the comb, the stroking of his hands, set up a tingling in her scalp that just made her want to purr. He knew it, too. He was taking his time about it, pampering her, bathing her in luxurious physical attention.

Yep. Foreplay. Definitely.

"Beautiful," he murmured when he'd combed it all smooth. "Like black silk." He divided it and draped it over both shoulders. She felt his fingertips rub the row of little vertebrae at the top of her spine, as if their shapes fascinated him. She felt his breath, hot and ticklish on the sensitive skin there. "You smell so good." Did she hear the words or just feel them, whispered against her nape? "I never thought baby powder could smell so good."

She couldn't move, couldn't breathe. She waited, strangely immobilized, her senses excruciatingly heightened, her eyes squeezed shut, until she felt what she had been waiting for....

His lips, hot and soft and excruciatingly gentle on the back of her neck. It was the heat that most astonished her. She felt seared, despite the tenderness of the kiss.

Her heart thudded in her chest as he pressed a second, and third, and fourth scalding, whisper-light kiss to her neck, which she'd never thought of as an erogenous zone, but that just showed what she knew, because every time his lips touched her, she felt it in every cell of her body, every inflamed, quivering inch of her, and this was just the start, there would be more...much more....

He backed off slightly, his hands on her upper arms, and paused. She opened her eyes; things spun, just a little. She focused on his image in the mirror, and everything stood still.

Emma understood the rules, even if she'd never played the game—unless you counted high-school make-out sessions with awkward adolescent boys, which she didn't. Gage Foster wasn't awkward, and he was no boy. He'd made his move. Now was her chance to put a halt to things, if she was so inclined. If she didn't, he would assume she wanted the same thing he did.

Did she? Did she really?

Emma closed her eyes. She saw the birthday cake with the thirty candles, heard her mother's voice: *Virginity's not a healthy condition...not at your age.*

She thought about Gage Foster's List of Admirable Character Traits, let it scroll through her mind.

Yes, she thought. *Yes.* He was the perfect candidate for the task at hand. He was good-looking and honorable and brave and sexy....

"I'm leaving the day after tomorrow," he said.

That, too.

"Zara? Did you hear me?"

Her eyes blinked open; she felt dizzy.

Zara. Right. The man she intended to lose her virginity to thought she was her sister. There was no way to feel good about that, even in her present half-inebriated—all right, mostly inebriated—state. Every time she was reminded of her leading role in this tawdry masquerade, she felt deceitful and frankly a little cheap, but what choice did she have? Even assuming she could convince him of her true identity, an unlikely prospect given his unwillingness to believe her, would that really be such a good idea at this point? There were a limited number of reactions with which he might greet this revelation, none of them pleasant, and all virtually guaranteed to ruin whatever chance she might have of shedding that pesky virginity by the time she had to face down those thirty candles.

"I'm flying back to Arkansas Wednesday," he said quietly to her reflection in the mirror. "You know how I feel about this town. Nothing could keep me here any longer than that." He looked as if he were searching for better words; finally, with a resigned expression, he said, "Nothing."

Emma nodded. "I understand."

This is a good thing, she told herself, perhaps just a tad too forcefully. *A good thing.* He'd be gone in two days. She could keep up the disguise that long; any longer, and she didn't think she'd have the stomach for it.

He was being a gentleman and making sure she knew this would just be a casual tryst, short-lived and meaningless. Good. That's all she was in the market for, after all. A physical encounter, devoid of troublesome emotions—quick, uncomplicated, tidy.

So, good. Good. This was a good thing.

"I just wanted to make sure," he said, "that I wasn't misleading you about...my intentions."

Emma drew in a deep, steadying breath and forced a smile. "I should think our intentions are pretty much on an even par."

Gage hesitated just briefly, his expression indecipherable, before returning her smile. "That's good." He trailed his hands down her arms, detoured them to her bare thighs. "'Cause I'd hate to have to rein myself in now."

"Don't rein yourself in," she said huskily.

He laughed softly. "I was hoping you'd say that." Sliding his hand up along her leather-encased hips, he said, "I'm as happy as a boy with a speckled pup and a new red wagon." He closed his hands lightly around her waist and urged her against him, so that her back rested against his chest; his legs, one updrawn, the other relaxed, more or less flanked her.

Emma saw them in the mirror—her nestled against him as he nuzzled her hair, his arms moving to encircle her. He felt so strong, seemed so sure of himself, so in control.

That's one of us.

She stuck her legs out in front of her and regarded her gauze-festooned knees with dismay. "I look like a little girl who's fallen off her tricycle."

"I don't know too many little girls who can fill out leather like you do." Tucking her hair behind her, he lightly trailed the fingertips of both hands down over her breasts and back up.

Emma watched in fascination as he caressed her, his touch so featherlight she could barely feel it; but she could see it—the sensual dance of his hands, the intensity of his gaze as he watched his own actions in the mirror. Her breasts seemed to swell within their confining satin bra and tight little jacket. She watched herself close her hands over his. He squeezed her aching flesh as he pressed himself against her; she felt, against the small of her back, the unmistakable evidence of his desire for her.

This is it, she thought, feeling branded where the rigid column had rubbed against her, through their layers of clothes. *This is really happening.* Would it hurt? she wondered, biting her lip. Could she pull off the pretense that she'd done it all hundreds of times before?

Gage reached up and stroked her bottom lip. He probably meant it to be soothing, but the caress of his callused fingertip on such sensitive flesh was breathlessly erotic.

"One of these days," he said, "you're gonna draw blood from biting this."

She twisted around to face him, one eyebrow cocked. "Blood?"

He grinned as he tilted her chin up and lowered his mouth to hers. "Just tryin' to get your attention."

Their lips met, heat against heat, deliciously sweet and wet and perfect. He took it slow, didn't push, didn't force her beyond a leisurely, intoxicating caress of their mouths. It was she—much to her surprise—who lightly prodded the seam of his lips with the tip of her tongue, inciting a low moan from him, a firmer pressure, a deeper, more impassioned kiss.

His hands raked her hair, molded her breasts, pulled her to him, hard. She wrapped her arms around him, wanting him closer, impossibly close.

Things reeled dizzyingly as he swept the pillows and throw from the chaise and shifted them both from vertical to horizontal with a few smooth moves. Emma shut her eyes to help fight off the wave of vertigo this adjustment spawned. When she opened them, she was lying on her back with Gage reclining next to her, his weight resting on an elbow.

"You okay?" he asked, smoothing her hair off her face. "You looked a little peaked for a second there. And from the way you're talkin', you're soundin' a little...fuzzy around the edges."

She *was* slurring; she'd have to watch that. "Just a little delayed stress from the subway, I guess," she lied, not wanting to let on that she'd been surreptitiously tossing back the ol' Dr. Daniels as premedication for her imminent deflowering.

"You've had a rough day." Thoughtfully he stroked her cheek, then her throat. "We don't have to..." He indicated the chaise longue, and them, with a sweep of his hand. "You know. We don't. I mean, I don't want to take advantage of you—"

"Is it all right if I take advantage of *you*?" Curling a hand around his neck, she lowered his head and kissed him, scarcely believing that she, Emma Sutcliffe—dweeb extraordinaire, perennial virgin, Our Lady of the Panic Attacks—was actually grabbing a man, a man she'd met that very day, and kissing him. Like she meant it. And, wonder of wonders, she did.

"I'm yours for the taking," he murmured against her lips. He kissed her again, with enthusiasm, one hand snaking down to cup a breast while he settled himself on top of her, hips snugged together, his long, denim-clad legs twined with hers. He moved against her in a lazily carnal rhythm, to which her body responded with escalating urgency. Her hips moved in sync with his; her breath quickened; she clutched at his shirt.

"You are so beautiful," he whispered raggedly, "and so sexy." He kissed her throat; she threw her head back, delirious with pleasure and anticipation.

He released her breast to scoop a hand under her bottom and lift her toward him. Cradling him between her thighs now, her skirt having ridden up, she felt, against the damp satin of her panties, the unyielding ridge of his erection, impelling her stroke by stroke toward a heart-pounding climax.

Movement in the mirror drew her attention. She saw them locked together, his body straining sinuously—hers, too, as she approached a crisis of pleasure she'd never experienced with a man. The sight yanked her abruptly back to earth, just when she'd been about to leave it. How could she go that far—lose herself so completely—in the arms of this man she hardly knew? Suddenly she felt exposed, rawly vulnerable. Losing her virginity to Gage Foster she could handle; achieving satisfaction with him—writhing and moaning and losing control—she couldn't. It was too much, too personal. If this was a panic attack, so be it, but she just couldn't.

"Gage." She pushed against him, trembling, gathering her wits. "Gage, stop. I can't...I can't."

"What's wrong, sweetheart?"

"I just can't—you know. I can't."

"Have you ever..."

"Yes, but—"

"Then you can."

"But—"

"Look at me." Gage gathered her in his arms, compelled her with his steady gaze to meet his eyes. "You're safe with me. You can let go with me." He continued rocking against her, the movement languid, mesmerizing, oddly comforting, and still—despite her anxiety—intensely arousing. "You're so beautiful and so sexy. I just want you to come. I want to make you come. Now, like this...."

Emma closed her eyes, felt the weight of him, the intoxicating pressure of his body against hers.

"And then again later," he breathed against her lips, "when I'm inside you." He kissed her softly. "But first like this. Just you, like this. I want to see your face when you come...."

He kept on in that vein, whispering provocative things no man had ever whispered to her before in that deep, soothing drawl, pushing against her, coaxing her closer and closer to fulfillment.

She felt it gathering, felt her heart swelling painfully, her entire body taut and shuddering. He held her tight, murmuring, "That's right. Let go. Just let go."

When it happened, he closed his mouth over hers, muffling her cries. She bucked beneath him with astonished pleasure. It roared through her, rocking her with its force.

"Ah," he said quietly as her climax diminished. "Yes.

That was so sweet. You're so beautiful, so responsive. I want you so much—more than ever now." He kissed her cheek as she lay panting and overwhelmed and vaguely stunned. "And you know what?"

She looked up at him, hovering over her with a boyish smile on his way-too-handsome face. "What?"

"The best is yet to come." He kissed the tip of her nose. "But first—" he rolled off of her and stood "—I need to get something." He reached down to brush his knuckles over her cheek, then crossed to the bathroom, closing the door behind him.

Emma sat up, dazed and sweat dampened and struggling to keep the room from swimming in different directions. She noticed her reflection in the mirror and smiled. Her face was flushed, her eyes sparkled, her clothes and hair were in complete disarray. She looked like she'd been having *way* too good a time.

"The best is yet to come," she informed her reflection with a bleary smile. Standing awkwardly, she stretched her back, her gaze on the bathroom door. Emma knew what Gage had gone to get, of course. It was a good thing *he'd* thought of protection—and had some at hand, apparently—because it had, foolishly, been the last thing on her mind.

Protection. Condoms. Emma realized she was nibbling on that bottom lip, and forced herself to stop. Would he put it on, or would he expect her to? Could she fake expertise at something she'd never done before? The mechanics of prophylactics—not to mention the entire sexual act—suddenly struck her as unfathomable. Oh, she'd read the how-to books with the semitasteful, soft-focus drawings of wholesome couples pretzeled together in presumed ecstacy, but lacking any actual hands-on experience, as it were, could she pull off the pretense that she knew what she was doing? Or would she look like an idiot?

Crossing on unsteady legs to the table, she tilted the bottle of Jack Daniels over her glass and poured. And kept right on pouring.

GAGE CURSED A BLUE STREAK as he rummaged through his toilet kit. "Where the hell are you when I need you?" he growled, upending the kit and dumping its contents all over the vanity. His badger shaving brush and vitamin jar rolled onto the floor.

"Damn and double damn." Where were they? It had been months since he'd last used them, but he could swear they were in there. He sorted through his meager toiletries, spreading them out, taking his time, wondering what, exactly, he was doing anyway, and thinking maybe it was all for the best, this was probably a bad idea.

He'd known her for what? A few hours? He'd never in his life gone to bed with a woman on such short acquaintance. All right, once, but he'd been sixteen and it had been Tijuana and his first time, and it had cost him a month's allowance.

Okay, twice if you counted that redhead in Fort Worth who'd jumped him in the Crawfords' pantry while they were singing "Happy Birthday" in the dining room.

But those had been two isolated and unrepresentative episodes. In general Gage Foster was really not a very big fan of casual sex. Of course, he wasn't too keen on commitment, either; when he finally married, it was going to be for real, like with his parents, not one of these try-her-on-for-size deals. Having found the vast borderland between one-nighters and till-death-do-us-part rife with land mines of one sort and another, his sex life consisted essentially of one long dry spell punctuated by the occasional short-term relationship based on guess what.

Another thing, Gage mused as he arranged and rear-ranged the items strewn on the vanity. Zara Sutcliffe wasn't exactly his type, not by a long shot. At thirty-nine, his tastes were pretty well set. He knew what he liked: real women; honest, dependable, down-to-earth women who didn't play games and get all het up over nothing. Pretty was a given; he liked them pretty—to pretend otherwise would be dishonest—but he didn't like the kind of pretty that came out of a bottle, never had. He thought the sexiest thing a woman could wear was a white T-shirt and a pair of Levi's, the button-fly kind. He loved undoing those buttons; even thinking about it got him hard.

What he'd always disliked in a woman was artifice of any kind. Hair spray turned him off. Ditto Ringling Brothers makeup. And clothes that made a woman look like she couldn't take a full breath.

Gage pictured Zara Sutcliffe in her snug, yellow leather suit and thought, well, maybe it was okay if *he* was the one who had trouble breathing.

Zara Sutcliffe. Lenny Bruce once said the perfect woman was a cross between a stripper and a kindergarten teacher. That was a pretty fair description of Zara Sutcliffe, and he had to admit, he was *way* more taken with her than he should be, given he'd only just met her. And given that whole weird evil-twin thing, which, thankfully, she seemed to have abandoned.

She was an enigma, plain and simple—a fusion of sweet and sexy that spun his wheels faster than they'd been spun in a long time. Her responsiveness, once she'd relaxed enough to let go of herself, had excited him intensely. He was used to women who'd ridden around the paddock a few times; when it came to sex, they went through the well-rehearsed motions. Zara, on the other hand, seemed to drink up everything they did together, as if the whole thing were a process of discovery and not the same old same old. There was something almost touching about that sensual wonderment. Only thing was, he couldn't quite figure out how a sexually experienced woman could still be so endearingly naive.

She was a woman who wore black garter belts and stockings...but couldn't quite figure out how to take them off. Nothing about her made good sense, yet everything about her turned him on.

Strangely enough, it was her sweetness that got to him most. She had a kind of insightful innocence he'd never encountered before. It made him want to wrap himself around her.

And bury himself deep inside her.

Ah! There was a little half-hidden compartment inside the toilet kit that he rarely used. Gage grabbed the kit and unzipped the compartment. "Gotcha!" He slid out the strip of condoms, grinning in anticipation, his misgivings vaporizing in a heartbeat.

He flung open the bathroom door to find Zara leaning against the little table in the middle of the room, a glass to her mouth. When she saw him, she lowered it; about a finger of bourbon remained in it. She blinked at the strip of condoms in his hand and then swiftly chugged down the rest of her drink.

"Whoa." Shoving the condoms in his back pocket, he crossed to her in two strides, confiscated the glass and screwed the top back on the bottle. "Looks like we're down a quart," he said, inspecting the level of bourbon remaining. "How much have you had to drink?"

"I'm jus' trying to...you know. Relax." Her eyes shifted in an obvious struggle to focus on him.

Uh-oh. "Zara, Zara, Zara."

"What?"

"Sweetie, it looks to me like you may have gotten...a little too relaxed."

"What do you mean?" she asked thickly. "I'm fine. I feel great." She waved her arm, almost throwing herself off balance. "Great!"

"That's terrific." He grabbed her arm to keep her from falling. "I'm very happy for you."

"Don't patronize me." She shook him off, turned and walked slowly back to the chaise longue, her movements very deliberate and oddly graceful in the manner of one determined to appear sober despite a stratospheric blood-alcohol concentration.

How had this happened without his catching on? He'd had other things on his mind, that's how. Even so, Zara's inebriation had obviously snuck up on her. You'd think a woman like her would be acclimatized to alcohol, but then she seemed to be just full of surprises.

This, of course, was one of her more unpleasant ones, he reflected as she staggered in slow motion to the chaise and sank down on it. Closing her eyes, she swayed ever so slightly.

"Damn."

She squinted at him. "What?"

He made himself smile as he walked toward her. "Damn, you're pretty."

"I thought you din' like to swear in front of me."

He sat next to her and curled an arm around her shoulder. "I don't, but you make me forget myself."

"Yeah?"

"Yeah. Close your eyes."

"Why?"

"'Cause I'm gonna lay you down, and I don't want you to get dizzy."

"Oh," she said, as if this made perfect sense, which in fact it did.

She closed her eyes. He lowered her gently onto her back. When she tried to open her eyes, he whispered, "Shh. Keep them closed. Just for a minute."

"Why?" she mumbled.

"It's a surprise. You'll see." He stroked her face lightly, and then her throat, as her breathing slowed.

"When's the s'prise coming?"

"Soon. Just relax."

Within about sixty seconds, her breathing was deep and steady. "Zara," he whispered. No response. He thumbed open an eyelid. She was out for the count.

"Surprise," he murmured. He kissed her cheek for no very good reason except that he felt drawn to do it. Then he went over to the big four-poster bed, pulled down the covers to expose the white cotton bottom sheet, and plumped the pillows.

"Okay, sweetheart, it's bedtime." He lifted her like a baby, marveling at how light she was, and laid her on the bed.

And then he stepped back and assessed the situation.

She was still fully dressed. He could leave her that way, but that suit was tight and it was leather and he just couldn't see it. So he'd have to undress her. At least partially. No two ways about it, he had to take her clothes off. Shoot, he had an obligation to do it.

So do it.

He sat on the edge of the bed and took hold of the jacket's scooped neckline to unsnap it, his fingers sliding beneath the garment's silken lining and the warm, unbelievably soft upper slopes of her breasts.

But be cool about it. You're a doctor, remember?

Ex-doctor.

Whatever, be cool.

Pop. Pop. The top two snaps released and the leather sprang open, revealing a minimal black satin bra ornamenting just about the jauntiest little round breasts he'd ever seen.

Dr. Foster took a deep, calming breath and popped open the remaining snaps. Rolling her gently from side to side, he managed to remove the jacket, which he hung over the back of a chair.

She had square little shoulders with just the right amount of muscle, elegant collarbones, those too-perfect breasts that made his hands itch—*you're a doctor, you're a doctor*—and a nice, delicate little waist. Slender but very, very feminine. Just right.

She stirred, mumbled something and then quieted.

Now for the skirt. It snapped up the front, too. Gage flexed his fingers.

Pop.

Pop.

Pop.

Hmm. More black satin.

Pop.

Pop.

He opened the skirt, now just a rectangle of yellow leather lined in matching silk, with some darts in it for shape. She wore tiny little black satin drawers that barely covered what they needed to, and a matching garter belt, sans stockings, of course.

Jeez, Louise. Woman, couldn't you have waited till later to get falling-down drunk? Trying not to think about what could have been, Gage gingerly slid the skirt from beneath her.

She muttered something. It sounded like "Two mill'n dollars, who'd pay two mill'n dollars for that?"

Gage had gotten the skirt mostly out from under her when she grumbled something unintelligible and rolled away from him, onto her side.

He gaped. Those little drawers didn't even cover what they *needed* to in back. All there was was a kind of narrow triangular strip that ran from the waistband down to...well, down to where you couldn't see it anymore. On full and glorious display was a truly spectacular butt, small and tight and dimpled, the nicest he'd seen outside of a girlie magazine.

Damn thing looks like it's been airbrushed.

Part of him wished he had a camera. Another part wished, yet again, that she hadn't gone and gotten herself swacked before he had a chance to get better acquainted with her really very impressive butt.

The moral and upstanding part of him—well, more than one part of him was upstanding right now, but the part of him that still had some grip on propriety—tossed the skirt onto the chair, pulled the covers up over her, grabbed one of the pillows and the coverlet and dumped them on the chaise longue.

Can't figure out what went wrong, he thought as he stripped down and settled in on the narrow little couch, his feet hanging off the end, knowing he'd never get comfortable here and resigning himself to a long, sleepless night thinking about you know who and you know what.

I said, "Pretty please."

6

GAGE WOKE UP, so he knew he must have finally gotten to sleep. It was dark in the room, because of those heavy velvet drapes, but it felt like morning. Hearing muffled sounds, he shifted, every bone in his body aching from way too long a night on way too short a "bed." A ribbon of light glowed at the bottom of the bathroom door.

She was awake. He felt around listlessly in the heap of clothes on the floor next to him until he located his watch and squinted at it: 7:14. There was a lamp on a little table nearby, and he stretched to turn it on. Tossing aside the coverlet, he lowered his feet to the carpet, groped around for his boxer shorts and stood to shake them out.

"Oh!"

Gage turned to find Zara in the open doorway of the bathroom, looking pretty as hell—if a tad pale—with a white bath towel wrapped around her and her hair wet and combed back. Sweet-scented steam wafted out around her.

Color suffused her face as she scanned the length of his naked body, and then she abruptly wheeled around. "I'm sorry, I didn't mean to—"

"Don't worry about it," he drawled groggily, stepping into the shorts and pulling them up. "I'm not bashful." But she was, he noted with interest as she nervously tucked her towel in tighter. She was completely flummoxed. Not quite how he would have expected Zara Sutcliffe to react—especially after last night. "How are you feeling?"

"My stomach's bothering me, and I've got a headache."

"I'm not surprised."

"How did you sleep?" she asked stiffly. Something *was* bothering her. Maybe she didn't remember everything that happened last night; or maybe she *did*.

"Just dandy," he lied. He *would* have slept fine—he'd slept in worse places, God knew—if only he hadn't spent hour after hour lying there with a blue-steel hard-on, thinking about her underneath those sheets in about half an ounce of black satin and nothing else. "You can turn around now," he said. "I got all the scary parts covered up."

Zara cast him a droll look as she turned to face him, her arms wrapped tightly around her waist. "I'm finished in there," she said, nodding toward the bathroom. "It's all yours if you want it. I'll just get dressed out here."

Even half-awake, Gage knew she was angling for some privacy. Muttering his thanks, he pulled a clean pair of shorts out of the dresser and padded to the bathroom, closing the door behind him. He laid his fresh underwear on the vanity next to something gold—her earrings, he saw, lifting one to examine it. It was heavy, with dangling bits that rattled softly as he turned it this way and that. Despite his aversion to artifice in women, he did have a weakness for big earrings like this, the kind that tickle a woman's shoulders.

Something black and glimmery hung on the inside of the door—her underthings. He plucked them off, intrigued by their airy seductiveness. There wasn't much to the panties, and the garter belt held no surprises, but that perky little bra was just a marvel of structural engineering. In the midst of his dopey ruminations on the mysteries of intimate attire in the 1990s, it occured to him that Zara would probably need these.

He cracked open the door and peeked out. She was standing near the bed with her back to him, wearing the little yellow skirt and shrugging the jacket on over her bare back.

She must have sensed him watching her, because she turned around, holding the jacket closed with both hands. "Yes?"

"You...left these in here." He held the undergarments out to her. "I thought you might, uh...want them." Although she'd gotten dressed without them. For the life of him, Gage couldn't keep himself from...hell, he was *leering* at her, inspecting her up and down while he tried to internalize the fact that she wasn't wearing a single thing—not a stitch—under that provocative little outfit. Even the skinned knees didn't compromise the effect.

She bit her lip; she really should cut that out.

"I just showered," she said, blushing again. "I didn't want to put on yesterday's underwear after I'd showered."

"Right. Okay. Sure. Just checking." Gage closed the bathroom door and rested his forehead against it. "Go away," he muttered at the erection straining his boxers. "Come back when I've got a job for you. Until then, you're off the payroll."

He could, of course, simply waltz back in there, in all his tumescent eagerness, and try to take up where they'd left off last night—a tempting scenario, but one riddled with pitfalls. If she didn't remember what happened last night, she'd probably slap him for coming on to her this morning. If she did remember, then she most likely regretted it, judging from how stressed-out she seemed, and wouldn't be in any mood for a reenactment.

The prudent course of action was to shock this pesky boner into submission with a nice, cold shower and banish all libidinous thoughts from his mind until such time as he and the singular Ms. Sutcliffe parted company. As play-mates went, she wasn't that smart a choice to begin with, seeing as how she had designs on him as a client and—

She wasn't wearing any underwear.

He barely knew her—

Not a stitch.

Gage twisted the cold water on in the shower, kicked off his shorts and got in.

He sucked in an astonished breath as frigid water pum-meled him. Every nerve in his body shrieked, *This sucks! Stop this now!*

Swearing with a vehemence and creativity he hadn't known he possessed, he grabbed the faucet and cranked heat into the water until his heart slowed down and he could breathe normally again. "Guess I showed *you*," he muttered, glaring down at the meekly flaccid organ that had goaded him into his first—and last—cold shower.

No, that was wrong, he thought as he soaped up. It was Zara who'd driven him beneath the icy spray, Zara herself. It didn't matter what she wore or didn't wear. It didn't mat-ter that she'd tried to dupe him with that loony twin story, or almost got him killed, or drank herself into a stupor that cost him what had promised to be a night of deliciously wanton excess, just when he was about to turn forty and could use a good dose of that.

The fact was, something sparked between them that he'd never felt, not to this extent anyway, with anyone else, and that spark had ignited in record time. Twenty-four hours ago, he hadn't even met her in the flesh. Now here he was, wishing she'd up and move to Arkansas so he could see whether that spark had a chance to turn into a flame.

Right. Hotshot literary superagents didn't live in log houses just outside of Backscratch, Arkansas. He'd known that all along; it was a given. And grumpy old surgeons turned hack writers who upchucked at the sight of spit on a sidewalk did not move to New York City, no way José. It wasn't gonna happen. It didn't even have a chance. He'd best quit ruminating on it; there just wasn't any point.

Gage located the little bottle of hotel shampoo, which Zara had half emptied, and lathered up his hair.

He'd hated having to make that I'm-leaving-the-day-after-tomorrow speech, but he would have felt like a heel if he hadn't set the record straight on that particular score before things got to the sweaty and breathless stage. Of course, the joke was on him; once things got to that stage, they'd kind of stalled out.

Serves me right for even coming to this town, he thought as he rinsed off. *Things never go right here. Come 5:20 tomorrow afternoon, I'm getting on that plane, and this time nothing will ever sucker me back. Nothing.*

"ARE YOU FEELING BETTER?" Gage asked as he polished off the steak and eggs he'd ordered in the posh hotel dining room.

Disgraced, debased and degraded. "A little," Emma mumbled into her coffee cup as she tried to avoid looking at the butter-slathered English muffin on her plate. *I will never live down my humiliation. It will haunt my dreams until the end of time.*

"Did you sleep okay at least?" he asked.

"I slept like a stone." *And woke up in my underwear.*

"That's good." He motioned to the waitress for their check. "I was worried, you know, because of, well..."

"Because of how much I drank."

He nodded.

"Look, I'm really embarrassed about that."

"No need to be embarrassed."

No need to be embarrassed about getting drunk and...doing

what she'd done with him? "That's never happened to me before." *None of it.* "I never, um, lost control like that."

A knowing flicker in his eyes told her he'd caught the subconscious double entendre. "Losing control once in a while is a healthy thing. Everyone should let loose periodically. It's like releasing a little steam from the valve."

"Yeah, well, I think I may have blown a gasket last night."

"I liked it." He smiled. "A lot."

That was reassuring, but since she had no desire whatsoever to explore in conversation with Gage Foster the subject of last night's frolics on the chaise longue, Emma changed the subject. "I'm going home now—to my house in Queens. Thank you for breakfast. Thank you for... everything. For saving my life."

"You already thanked me for that." He clicked the pen the waitress handed him and signed for their meal.

"It's the kind of thing you're allowed to thank someone for more than once," she insisted. "It's a pretty big deal, when someone jumps in front of a train to save you. I just wanted you to know that I think you're..."

He looked up, his gaze riveted on her. The waitress reached for the slip and the pen; he handed them over without looking away from Emma.

You're funny and passionate and smart and sexy, and I'm crazy about you. "You're a good man," Emma said quietly. "There aren't too many of them around. I haven't met too many, anyway."

"Thanks." He still hadn't stopped looking at her with those hypnotically blue eyes of his.

"I've got to go," she managed to say, rising from the table and plucking the gold raincoat off the back of her chair. She glanced around for her bag before remembering that it was gone and she'd probably never see it or its contents again. Well, she'd managed to get along without it for what—a good sixteen, seventeen hours already. As cold-turkey withdrawals went, this really wasn't so bad. She missed her underwear a little bit more, but in a way it was kind of...exciting, not having any on. The silk lining of her suit felt heavy and slick and sexy against her bare flesh. She felt daring, in a way, and it felt good.

Gage stood when she did, looking decidedly pensive.

She stuck out her hand as he came around the table toward her; he automatically took it. "Goodbye," she said. "I wish..."

"What?" He whispered it, his hand tightening around hers.

She bit her lip. He gripped her hand harder.

"I wish we could have gotten to know each other better." Trust her to finally feel this way about someone—under these impossible circumstances.

"Me, too." He didn't let up on her hand; there was something almost desperate in his eyes, as if it panicked him to think of her turning and walking away. "It's funny. Usually I don't...I mean, you're not the type of woman I would usually...want to get to know better. Not that I generally run into women like you. We don't grow that many down where I come from. The thing is, and don't take this the wrong way, but I didn't really expect to like you. Much less..."

Emma felt her heart quicken.

"Zara..."

Zara. Right. "Goodbye, Gage." Forcibly pulling her hand from his grip, she turned and wove her way through the dining room, crossed the lavish lobby and stepped out into the bright morning sunshine.

"Cab, miss?" asked the doorman, a dead ringer for Scotty from *Star Trek.*

"Uh..." She didn't even have a buck to tip this guy, much less money for a cab.

"Zara!"

Turning, she saw Gage jogging through the front door of the Plaza. "How are you going to get to Queens? You don't have any money."

She sighed. "I'd like to say I have a plan, but I don't."

He nodded resolutely. "I'll take you." Turning to Scotty, he said, "Can we get a cab?" The doorman raised a white-gloved hand and a taxi materialized in front of them, as if by transporter beam. He lowered the hand, palm up, for the proffered tip.

Gage guided Emma into the back seat and slid in after her. "We're going to Flushing, Queens," he told the cabbie.

"Address?" he asked.

Emma stammered out her address, and the cab screeched away from the curb. She turned to Gage. "You don't have to do this."

"Sweetheart, there's not much in life a body *has* to do. There's plenty a body *ought* to do, if he wants to hold his head up. I can't just let you go home alone. You don't know what you're gonna find there. That guy could be there."

She shook her head. "If he was gonna rip me off, he would have done it and left by now."

"You sound pretty sure of yourself."

"He wouldn't stick around," she insisted. "It doesn't fit the psychological profile. Burglars like to do their work at night, as quickly and quietly as possible, and then get out of there. It's too risky to wait around."

"Yeah, but this isn't just any garden-variety burglar," he noted. "This guy pushed you in front of a moving train, so we know he's capable of murder. For no good reason."

"It's true," she conceded, "that capricious acts of violence don't fit neatly into the burglar profile, but if we factor in the likelihood of narcotics abuse, and merge the erratic brutality of the hard-core drug addict with the stealth of the—"

"Whoa. Where'd you learn all this criminal-psychology stuff?"

"From books. I like to read about police work and private investigation."

"Research for that cozy mystery of yours?"

"If I ever write it."

"You will." He took her hand, and she let him hold it all the way to Flushing.

"OH, GOD." Emma swayed in the open front door of her house, actually dizzy from the shock of what had been done to her living room. The raincoat, which she had been carrying, slid off her arm, the ray gun within clattering onto the concrete stoop.

"Don't faint on me, sweetheart." Gage banded his arms around her and drew her close. Slumping against him, she shut her eyes and concentrated on the soothing drawl rumbling from his chest. "You can handle this. You *can*. You're strong. Say it."

"I'm strong," she groaned halfheartedly.

"I'm tough," he prompted. "I'm the famous, invincible Zara Sutcliffe. Go ahead."

"I'm...gonna have to sit down."

Gage led her on rickety legs to her frayed old ottoman, which, like most of the rest of her furniture, had been overturned. Supporting her with one hand, he grabbed the upholstered stool by one of its scarred wooden legs and righted it.

"You shouldn't touch that," she said as he gently lowered her into a sitting position on the ottoman. She kept her knees together, mindful of her lack of underwear beneath this all-too-short skirt. "We shouldn't touch anything. Fingerprints."

"I don't mean to touch anything else," he said, scanning the chaos of her ransacked home, "except maybe the phone, so we can call this in to the cops." Emma followed his gaze as it lit on the shabby wallpaper, torn window shade and threadbare carpet. He peered down the corridor through the back door at the eyesore of an aboveground pool that took up most of the rear yard. She knew what he was thinking: high-and-mighty Zara Sutcliffe lives *here?*

"My portable phone's in here," she said. "Last I saw it, it was on the floor right there." She'd taken Zara's phone call from Australia. She recalled resisting the urge to hurl the receiver across the room, and laying it down carefully—in a spot now hidden beneath a pile of worn paperbacks.

Squatting down, Gage began digging through the books. "Did you just move in?" he asked, with a nod toward the cardboard cartons—Mysteries, *H-P*; Mysteries, *Q-T*—resting at odd angles all over the small room, their contents strewn in disorderly heaps.

"Yeah," she said distractedly as she took in the mayhem surrounding her. Bookcases lay facedown; her favorite one, which she'd just finished staining, was smashed. Her sewing box, two cartons of craft supplies and a carton of *CraftWorld* back issues had been, from all appearances, kicked open, their contents dumped unceremoniously among the scattered books.

"Are you sure the phone was here?" Gage asked, having had no luck finding it.

"That's where I put it."

"Maybe he stole it."

"It was a bargain-basement phone," she said. "It didn't even have autodial. He wouldn't have stolen it."

He cocked an eyebrow as he continued rooting through

the random debris that had once comprised her carefully ordered and meticulously cataloged world. "You almost sound like you know what you're talking about."

"I do!" she said archly.

He smiled. "Am I makin' you mad?"

"Yes!"

"Good. Keep those hackles up. You'll be less likely to keel over on me if you're ticked off. Ah!" He extricated the phone from beneath a mound of needlepoint canvas and handed it to her. "Here you go. I'll poke around a little, make sure whoever did this is gone."

"Remember—don't touch anything."

"Yes, Officer." He disappeared through the door to one of the two bedrooms, the one she was going to make into an office. "It's a disaster in here, but your fax machine's still on the desk," he called out.

"Really? Great!" That was three hundred dollars saved. "Is the message light blinking on my answering machine?"

"No."

MacGowan Byrne hadn't called back yet, then.

"He left the laptop, too," Gage yelled.

"Yes!" Two grand, and she'd have *had* to replace it; it was what she wrote on.

"Guess he doesn't like office equipment."

"Should be easy enough to fence. He probably didn't have a vehicle to put it in. Check my bedroom. I had some jewelry in a box in the bottom dresser drawer. Good stuff, all gold. He'll have taken that."

Gage left the office and walked into the bedroom. "Yikes."

"What?"

"He really tore things up in here."

Emma didn't want to see it, not yet anyway. She called information for the number of her local police precinct and dialed it. "Yes, I'd like to report a burglary," she told the voice on the other end. "Well, *like* may be too strong a word, but...what? Yes, I'll hold."

The voice connected her to another voice that connected her to a weary-sounding detective named Molloy, who took her name and address and asked for details. Emma related the encounter in the subway, and how she'd come home this morning to find the house trashed.

"Would you describe the missing items?" Molloy asked, to the muted clattering of a keyboard.

"Um..."

Gage came out from the bedroom with her jewelry box, whispering, "I found it on the floor—open." He tilted it to display its interior, and arched his eyebrows, as if to say, "What do you think of this?"

It was full. All the jewelry was there, every last bauble and bangle.

"Ma'am?" Molloy yawned. "The missing items?"

"Is there anything else I should be checking?" Gage whispered.

Emma shook her head, completely perplexed. That jewelry was portable, easily sold and worth thousands; she didn't own anything more valuable. The intruder had found it, opened it and left it. Why?

"Ma'am?"

"Yes, um...I'm sorry. I don't seem to be missing anything. In fact he left a whole boxful of gold jewelry sitting on the floor of my bedroom."

There was a pause. "Nothing was taken?"

"Apparently not."

The detective's answering sigh was long and eloquent. "So all we're talking about here is some vandalism."

"Well..." Emma looked around at the catastrophe that used to be her living room. "Quite a lot of vandalism."

She met Gage's gaze; he grimaced and closed the jewelry box, clearly discerning, as she did, that significant help would not be forthcoming from New York's finest.

"Do you have any enemies?" Molloy asked.

So police detectives actually asked that. Emma would have to remember that for her whodunit. "None," she answered. "Anyway, I just moved here. I don't know anybody. I'm sure it was the guy from the subway, the one who snatched my bag and pushed me onto the tracks."

"Yeah, but see," Molloy said tiredly, "it don't make sense that a crazed junkie would bother coming all the way from Manhattan to Flushing just to toss your furniture around. It was probably just a local teenager getting his kicks. If it happens again—"

"*Again?*" Emma clenched the phone so hard her hand hurt. "Can't you try and catch the guy—"

"Honestly? It'd be a waste of time. Like I said, if it happens again, give us another call. Have a nice day, Ms. Sutcliffe." He hung up.

Bolting to her feet with impotent frustration, Emma hauled back to pitch the phone across the room, but, true to dweebish form, hesitated.

"Go for it," Gage urged. "Only aim for the wall. Windows are harder to fix."

"But the phone might break."

"Good riddance. It doesn't even have autodial."

Yeah! Good riddance! Emma heaved that puppy as hard as she could. It sailed across the room and bounced harmlessly off the wall, landing on a blanket of strewn magazines.

"Feel better?" Gage asked, loping over to inspect the shallow dent in the wall and retrieve the phone.

"No."

Grinning, he checked the instrument for damage. "Never did work for me, either."

"Then why did you tell *me* to do it?"

"'Cause you were achin' to try it." Tucking the jewelry box under his arm, he punched the phone's On button and brought it to his ear. "You still got a dial tone."

"Swell." Steeling herself, Emma toured the small house. The intruder—she was still convinced it was the guy from the subway—had had a field day. In the kitchen, he'd taken stacks of dishes out of the cabinets and dumped them on the floor, cracking many of them. All the sheets and towels had been yanked out of the linen closet, unfolded and left in a mountain in the hallway. Her bedroom was the worst, though. He'd wrenched her mattress right off the bed-springs and shaken out the contents of every dresser drawer. She waded through the riot of tangled clothing, picking a few utilitarian items—jeans, a T-shirt, a sweat-shirt, some sneakers—and stuffing them into a small tote bag. She longed to get into her own clothes, but she balked at the idea of spending any more time here than absolutely necessary; she'd change later.

When she emerged from the bedroom, she found Gage standing by the window in the living room with her open jewelry box, sorting idly through its contents. He twirled an ornate Victorian-era gold bracelet adorned with a sprin-kling of diamonds and watched the sun spark off it. "Nice. Do you ever wear it?"

"I never wear any of it."

"Why not?"

She shrugged, then rubbed her arms, suddenly chilly. "My father gave it to me. But it belonged to my grand-mother, and I liked her, so I don't want to sell it."

Gage watched her closely, his expression sobering. He

replaced the bracelet in the box and closed it. Quietly he asked, "How bad was it?"

Emma drew in an unsteady breath. "He didn't beat me. Never laid a hand on me. So I guess I got off easy, huh?"

"There are lots of ways to ruin a kid's childhood. Which one did your father pick?"

"Can we not talk about this?" He'd breached enough of her defenses already; the subject of her and Zara's upbringing at John Sutcliffe's hands was still, after all these years and her father's death, an open emotional sore.

Gage nodded slowly. "Sure. But I want you to know that I wasn't asking out of...morbid curiosity. I care. I don't know why. I mean, we hardly know each other. Despite, you know...last night..."

Emma felt heat bloom on her face. "Can we please not talk about that, either?" Turning, she crossed to the open front door, scooped her raincoat up off the stoop and started struggling into it. "I want to get out of here."

"What about the locks?" he asked, coming up behind her and helping her with the coat. "Aren't you going to have them changed?"

She sighed. "Yeah, but not today. I really don't want to stick around here. And even if the locks are changed, I won't feel safe."

"I'll take you back to the Plaza," he said.

"No." Emma didn't think she could keep up the playacting. It had gone on too long already.

"Where will you stay?" he asked.

"At my..." *Sister's apartment.* That's what she'd been about to say. Should she try, one last time, to convince Gage of her true identity? She'd come to care an awful lot about him in an awfully short time, odd given that she'd never been impulsive before—far from it. Zara was right; Emma hated taking risks and had always kept her feelings under lock and key. But now they'd ambushed her. That might not be so bad, except that the object of her sudden affection a) thought she was someone else entirely and b) was flying back to Arkansas tomorrow, and she'd never see him again. Even if she *could* persuade him of the truth now, what would she gain? He'd still go back to Arkansas—he'd made it clear that nothing would keep him here—but he'd go back despising her for her dishonesty. She didn't think she could bear that.

"Zara?"

"My...mother lives on East 86th. A building called the Sans Souci. I'll go there."

He frowned in evident confusion. "Your mother lives in town? I thought you said you had no one to stay with."

"I didn't. She...it's a long story, but I didn't want to go there. There would have been questions, problems. I'm still not eager to face her, but—"

"Then come back to the Plaza with me." Smiling, he reached out and lightly stroked her cheek. "Pretty please?"

"No, I can't." It was time for the final curtain.

"Then how about dinner tonight?"

"No, it's...impossible."

His disappointment was obvious. He opened his mouth to speak, then seemed to think better of it. Finally he handed her the jewelry box. "Here, you'd best keep this with you." Taking her hand, he led her down the front steps. "I'll get a cab and take you to your mother's."

He held her hand in the cab until they got to East 86th and while they said goodbye in front of Zara's apartment building.

"I don't guess we'll be seeing each other after this," he said softly.

Emma shook her head, her throat tight.

"You know where I'm staying," he said. "Call me

if...well, for any reason. Even if you just want to talk." He threaded his fingers through her hair. "I wouldn't mind hearing your voice one more time."

Emma clutched the jewelry box to her chest and nodded.

His jaw clenched. "And you've got my number in Arkansas."

She nodded.

Gage sighed, bent his head to hers. He closed his eyes. Emma closed hers. His lips were so warm they made her eyes tear up. He prolonged the kiss, cupping her head with both hands while his mouth moved over hers so slowly, so tenderly. A man whistled as he passed them on the sidewalk; some teenage girls giggled.

Emma's heart ached. Her face was wet. Never in her life had she felt such an excruciating sense of loss.

MACGOWAN BYRNE SAT in a window booth at the Calypso Cafe on East 86th, washing down his third apple Danish with his fourth cup of coffee and waiting for the couple across the street to stop kissing. Man, they were really going at it. He couldn't blame the guy for his enthusiasm. Emma Sutcliffe was one tasty little piece—her and Zara both.

She was dressed the same as she'd been yesterday in the subway in a gold vinyl raincoat over a yellow leather suit. No way did she have the ray gun on her. All she had with her was one of those little canvas tote bags and her jewelry box, and she'd need something bigger to put the gun in—a suitcase, guitar case, something like that.

The jewelry box meant she'd definitely been to her house that morning. Mac would have sold his soul—what there was of it—to see the expression on her face when she opened her front door and saw his handiwork. Wait till she went up to her sister's apartment and discovered what was missing.

Mac had been a busy boy last night. After his fruitless tossing of that squalid little pit in Queens, he'd returned to Manhattan and broken into Zara's apartment to do the same. Only what he'd found there, perched on the couch watching a tape of *Blood Wedding*, surrounded by movie memorabilia that William would kill for, was the big prize herself, the one and only, mint-condition Candy Carmelle.

He'd recognized her immediately; damned if she didn't look the same—or nearly so—as when she was screaming her head off on the silver screen thirty years ago. The sight of her had confounded him, bringing back all those hours in front of the TV watching replays of *The Slithering* just for the scene where she's walking out of the lake in the shredded remains of that almost-transparent nightgown, her hair drenched but still perfectly coiffed, eyeliner and lipstick unaffected, breasts heaving with emotion beneath what was left of her sodden costume. Candy Carmelle had fueled Mac's fantasies for years, and suddenly here she was in her astoundingly abundant and preternaturally youthful flesh.

At first, all he could do was gape at her—until she tried to brain him with an electrode-studded head in a glass dome; *that* woke him up. He'd disarmed her, or rather disheaded her, during which she put up a surprisingly effective struggle. He demanded to know where the ray gun was hidden, and she swore it wasn't there; his gut told him she was telling the truth. Instinct took over then. Within about five minutes he had her bound and gagged in the trunk of his Jag. If William was willing to pay a cool two mill for that idiotic ray gun, how much more would he pay for Candy herself, given his obsession with her?

But one step at a time. First, Mac had to come up with the

ray gun. The lovely Ms. Carmelle might come in handy there. Then he could wipe the slate clean on that transaction and start on the next, even-more-profitable one. When the time seemed right, he'd offer William his ace in the hole—Candy Carmelle. Ten million didn't seem like too much to ask for a superbly well-maintained blond starlet from the sixties.

Mac swallowed the last of his coffee and signaled for the check just as the couple in front of the Sans Souci drew apart, hesitantly, it seemed. It was the cowboy from the subway station. He brushed his hand over Emma's face. Seeing her tears, Mac smiled. She was probably crying over what he'd done to her place. Or maybe she was still upset about the subway.

The waitress handed Mac the check. As he took it from her, he glanced with studied nonchalance around the coffeehouse, and then up and down the block as far as he could see through the window, searching for his perennial shadow. Things were trickier now that Mr. Big-shot G-man had started sniffing around. That bastard was making it his life's work to keep Mac from acquiring his collectibles by more...unorthodox means. Mac appeared to have thrown him off the scent for now, but he'd have to watch his step. He hated having to keep looking over his shoulder while he struggled to find that ray gun—one more tiresome complication.

Mac paid his bill and stood in the doorway of the Calypso, growling, "Come on come on come on," as Emma and the cowboy just stood there holding each other, for Chrissakes. Mac wondered about that guy. He'd been with Emma since yesterday. He was probably in on the ray gun scam; maybe he was even the brains behind it. This was starting to look like a conspiracy. Way too many people were becoming involved, all of whom would need to be deleted from the equation before Mac could rest easy.

In the meantime, there was probably plenty the cowboy could tell him, if Mac could get him in a talkative mood. Fingering the Indo-Persian dagger stuck in the waistband of his black linen trousers, he assessed the other man's potential for self-defense. He was as tall as Mac, and lean, and he moved like the kind of guy who could take care of himself, plus which he'd jumped in front of a subway train, which proved he had balls. But chances were he was unarmed, which gave Mac the edge.

"It's about time," Mac growled under his breath when lover boy and the twin finally—*finally*—called it quits on their little street-side soap opera. They turned away from each other more or less simultaneously. He walked away, dragging a hand through his hair. Emma stepped up to the front door of the Sans Souci. While the doorman was opening it for her, she turned to watch the cowboy walking away. Then she disappeared into the building.

Mac slid his mirror shades onto his face and stepped out onto the sidewalk. He walked west along 86th, keeping the cowboy in his line of sight. At the corner, he crossed over to the same side of the street and picked up his pace. He spotted an alley up ahead; perfect.

Speeding his gait up to a jog, he quickly overtook his prey, right in front of the alley. With one hand he grabbed the guy by his shoulder, stilling him; with the other, he pressed the tip of his dagger into his back through his corduroy jacket, hard.

"Mornin', cowboy," he said softly. "How about we step into my office and have a little chat?"

7

"YOU'RE OUT OF LUCK, buddy," Gage drawled as he was nudged by knifepoint into a dismal alley cluttered with trash cans and wooden crates; he smelled rotten vegetables and stale urine. "I've mostly got traveler's checks."

"I don't want your money."

Gage did not find it reassuring that his mugger had a mystery agenda; guy probably had at least one broken toy in the attic, which would make him all the harder to deal with. He'd known this kind of thing would happen if he kept coming back to this town.

The knifepoint eased up some. Gage turned around slowly, aiming for a sense of calm that would rub off on the nut with the knife, all the while thinking, *Why did it have to be a knife? Why couldn't it have been a gun, a baseball bat, a lead pipe, anything but a knife?* It had been his least-favorite form of weaponry since the attack at St. Vincent. He could barely stand to watch someone cut a steak; how was he supposed to keep his cool while he faced down a crazy mugger with a steel blade aimed at him?

The mugger wasn't quite what he would have expected. He was in his mid-thirties, maybe, and tall, with dark hair hanging loose past his shoulders. His clothes were black— baggy pants, silk shirt and leather jacket. The hand that held the knife—it was a bone-handled dagger, Gage saw— wore a Rolex, and from where he stood it looked like the real thing. The mirrored sunglasses were the perfect accessory. He looked like a TV coke dealer.

"Like I said," the guy purred. "All I want is to talk."

"Well, now," Gage said, eyeing the knife, "I'm afraid you've caught me at a bad time, partner, 'cause I'm not much in the mood for conversation right now." After his wrenching goodbye to Zara, that was no more than the truth.

"I'll make it easy on you. I'll ask questions, you answer. How does that strike you?"

"Like a line from a bad cops-and-robbers picture."

"Where's the ray gun?"

Gage kept his expression neutral as his mind ran a filmstrip of Zara taping that ridiculous chrome contraption inside her raincoat. "I'm sorry, did you say 'ray gun'?" he asked, going for a tone of mild incredulity.

He didn't see the punch coming, didn't expect a lightning jab in the stomach, leaving him doubled up and gasping. From the corner of his eye he saw his assailant lower the knife. Seizing his chance, he rammed his fist into the guy's ribs, sending him sprawling.

Gage tried to sidestep him, but the bastard stuck out a leg and tripped him. He landed faceup on cold concrete, the dagger pressed firmly against his throat. Son of a bitch was quick, Gage had to give him that.

The feel of steel pinching his Adam's apple did a real number on Gage's cool, although he tried not to show it. He wondered whether, if he'd seen the knife coming, he would have shielded his throat with his hand, like in the St. Vincent E.R. *No hands,* he silently commanded himself. *Anything but the hands.*

The mugger hovered over him, his hair hanging in his face, his entire body quivering, his expression one of fierce and singleminded concentration. He'd lost his shades in the scuffle, so Gage could see his eyes now. They were ghostly gold, with the feral gleam of the predator.

A memory ambushed him: Zara describing the guy who'd snatched her bag and thrown her in front of the train.... *His eyes, they were wolf's eyes...golden...savage.*

No...

"Save the theatrics, cowboy." Goldeneye stood up, clutching his side where Gage had punched him, and motioned with the dagger for Gage to rise. "This isn't the subway," he growled. "Your girlfriend's not here to impress."

Yes...the long hair, the height. What was going on here?

Gage gained his feet and bought a few seconds by making a show of dusting off his jeans as he tried to sort it all out. This was the guy who'd pushed Zara onto the tracks. But first he'd stolen her bag, probably thinking the ray gun was in it, never suspecting she had it taped inside her coat all along. No doubt he was also the one who'd redecorated Zara's house last night, searching for the gun.

The pieces didn't make a whole lot of sense—why would anybody go to those lengths over a toy gun?—but they added up to one crystal-clear conclusion: Zara was in danger, big-time. This guy was fixated, homicidal and at least a little deranged. And he was armed. With a knife, which gave Gage the sweats just thinking about it. His instinct was to get away from this lunatic and that blade as quickly as possible, but if he did that, the guy would be loose on the streets, and he'd probably go after Zara.

Gage had to make sure that didn't happen. Knife or no knife, he was going to have to take this clown out of circulation so he couldn't get to Zara. He'd have to immobilize him somehow and turn him over to the cops.

"I want that ray gun," Goldeneye rasped, the hand with the dagger shaking slightly, the other still gripping his side;

good, he probably had a couple of cracked ribs. "I want it very badly."

"Ask me if I give a national f—"

The knife whipped out. *No hands.* Gage ducked beneath the silver blur, rolled and leapt up as his opponent wheeled to face him. Darting sideways, Gage struck at the arm that held the dagger, hoping for a nice fractured radius. The bone didn't break, he could tell, but Goldeneye howled and dropped the knife.

Gage kicked the weapon under a Dumpster—*Yes!*—and swung again, grateful that skills honed during the tussles of his youth had managed to lurk in a forgotten cerebral nook this long. One blow connected with the guy's jaw, another with his eye.

His attacker stumbled back, his arms over his face; not what Gage would have expected from a knife-wielding bad-ass all dressed up in black. Clearly, he didn't like being hit, not in the head, anyway; that was good to know. Turning, Goldeneye lurched toward the Dumpster, threw himself down and started feeling around beneath it for the knife.

He had to be kidding. Gage was on him in a heartbeat. He yanked him to his feet and slammed him into a wall, sending metal trash cans toppling. Before the guy could raise his arms to protect himself, Gage landed another punishing blow to his head. As the shock of getting hit began to wear off, the creep started fighting back. Gage took a punch to the shoulder and one to the side of the head, but he shook them off; he was driven to stop this guy, had to stop him for Zara's sake.

A burst of pain in Gage's groin squeezed the air from Gage's lungs. *Bastard got me in the nuts!* Hard. His legs crumpled; his body curled automatically into a fetal position. Amid his breathtaking nausea, he was dimly aware of legs mov-

ing past him. The son of a bitch was getting away. With a
grunt of effort, Gage reached out and grabbed one of the
legs. Goldeneye stumbled, fell. As Gage struggled to rise,
the man in black grabbed the lid of a trash can, raised it
high and brought it down hard.

Gage's head exploded; that's what it felt like, a white-hot
eruption that consumed him in a blinding flash. Gradually
it receded, leaving his ears ringing, his head pulsing. His
groin still thudded with pain. He swallowed down the urge
to throw up.

With a monumental effort he managed to uncurl himself
and sit up. The alley was empty. *Nice goin', cowboy. You let
him get away.* Gage touched his throbbing forehead and felt
a nice, big lump sprouting. *You blew it, Foster. Now what do
you aim to do about it?*

There was only one thing to do, he reasoned as he rose
unsteadily to his feet and made his halting way out of the
alley. He had to get to Zara before Goldeneye did. Let her
know what kind of danger she was in, figure out how to
stop that bastard before he killed her over a toy gun, for
God's sake.

By the time he got to the Sans Souci, he was walking
fairly normally and his breathing had steadied. Nevertheless, the doorman—an enormous brute with a pencil mus-
tache, for pity's sake—gave him the evil eye as he held the
front door open. "May I help you, sir?"

"I'm here to see..." Shoot, he didn't know the mother's
name; well, she'd have the same last name, right? "Mrs.
Sutcliffe."

"*Ms.* Sutcliffe isn't home."

"Well, her daughter's here."

"Daughter?" The doorman cocked his head. A bald, be-
spectacled, sweat-suited man chatting with another tenant

at the bank of mailboxes turned and blinked at Gage. The jock was as burly as the doorman.

"Zara. Zara Sutcliffe. I just left her here," Gage insisted.

The doorman shook his head as if to clear it. "Ms. Sutcliffe—Zara Sutcliffe—went upstairs a few minutes ago, but then she came back down again right away and ran out the front door. She. Is. Not. At. Home."

Ran? "Are you sure?"

"I hailed her a cab myself." He swung the door open again. "Have a good day, sir."

"I'll have a dandy day if I can just figure out what's goin' on here. What's *Ms.* Sutcliffe's apartment number?"

"That's confidential information, sir."

"Besides," the bald guy interjected, "if you're really a friend of hers, how come you don't know her apartment number?" He took a couple of steps in Gage's direction, his chest puffed out and his massive arms curled at his sides in a fair imitation of a dominant male gorilla defending his turf.

Gage looked over the ape's shoulder, quickly scanning the names on the mailboxes until Sutcliffe popped out at him. Above the name was the apartment number: 7C.

"I'm afraid you're going to have to leave," the doorman told him.

"That's exactly what I wanted to hear you say," Gage responded. "Your employer will be very pleased."

"What?"

Gage withdrew his wallet and held up his fishing license as he backed away through the lobby in the direction of the elevator. "Sam Hill, Plaza Security Systems. The management hired me to check out the building and personnel for risk factors." He slapped the elevator's Up button. "They told me there'd be a bonus for every employee who followed proper security procedures. I'd say you qualify."

"A bonus?"

The elevator doors opened. "Fifty percent," Gage said as he stepped inside and stabbed the button for the seventh floor.

"Fifty percent?" the poor guy exclaimed as the doors closed and the elevator began its ascent. "Fifty percent of what?"

On the seventh floor, Gage was disconcerted to discover the door to apartment 7C standing ajar. He stepped inside and found himself in an elegant little foyer. Straight ahead was an open archway, on either side of which stood the requisite self-important columns, and beyond that...

Gage passed through the archway and found himself in...well, it had to be a living room, and for the most part it wasn't a bad-looking one, if a bit too modernesque for his taste. But not only was it littered with pop cans and dirty dishes, it was chock-full of the damndest knickknacks you'd ever want to see: eyeballs, rockets ships, monster masks.... There was a brain in a jar of green liquid that looked so realistic he thought for a second he was back in med school.

Old, yellowed movie posters were taped up all over the place, maybe just to cover up the bad paint job; the walls looked like someone had taken a spongeful of the wrong-color paint to them. Scanning the posters, Gage began to notice a common denominator: all of them costarred just about the best scream queen who ever shrieked her way into the hearts of adolescent males everywhere, the luscious Candy Carmelle. Something in one of the posters caught his eye.

"I'll be." It was the ray gun—the one taped inside Zara's coat—in the hands of the leading man of *Return of the Atomic Bride*. So the ray gun was a prop from an old movie from the sixties. Interesting, but it didn't explain why anyone would want to kill for it.

Advancing into the room, Gage noticed a black leather couch facing a big-screen TV in the corner. In front of the couch, a lacquered coffee table lay on its side. Stepping closer, Gage saw, on the carpet next to it...

"Whoa!" It took him a second—a couple of seconds—to catch his breath as he figured out that wasn't a real human head looking up at him from inside a glass dome; it was just another laugh-a-minute prop.

Gage looked around. A lamp with a crushed shade lay nearby. On the floor a couple of yards away was a silvery model of a rocket ship with a big dent in it. The evidence suggested a struggle. Had Zara been involved? Her mother?

Gage swiftly searched the apartment—the aggressively neomodern kitchen, white-on-white bedroom, disheveled guest room, marble bathroom and minuscule terrace hidden behind sliding glass doors and sheer curtains. It was empty. No Zara, no mother.

He took the elevator back downstairs, wondering how Zara Sutcliffe had managed to get so thoroughly under his skin in just twenty-four hours, why he couldn't shake this white-knight compulsion of his and when he would ever, *ever* learn to stop coming to this town. He raced through the lobby with the doorman screaming after him, "Fifty percent of what?" and flagged down a cab.

"Take me to the local police station."

An hour later, he left the station in disgust. He'd gone in talking about the ray gun, which, in retrospect, was a mistake. Their eyes had glazed over immediately and remained that way during the entire interview, except when they were exchanging looks. Yes, they said, the subway incident had been unfortunate, likewise the trashing of Zara's house and his mugging, but that was New York. Sure, he could report Zara Sutcliffe missing, but since she'd been "missing" for all of twenty minutes, he couldn't expect them to drop everything and tear the city apart looking for her, now could he? Sorry, but an overturned coffee table didn't necessarily indicate a struggle. They urged him to calm down. One of the cops actually asked him if he was on medication, and if so, had he skipped any pills lately?

Stopping at a pay phone, Gage called the Plaza Hotel and asked whether anyone had called and left a message for him, but no one had. Zara's office building was only a few blocks away, so Gage walked there. That squeaky little red-headed receptionist, Tina, told him her boss hadn't been back or called in since leaving yesterday afternoon one step ahead of him.

He hailed another cab and took it to Zara's house in Queens, thinking she might have gone home, after all. She'd neglected to relock the door that morning, so he had no trouble getting in, but she wasn't there. There were no messages on the machine.

It was midafternoon by the time he returned to the Plaza, crazed with worry. Zara had to be somewhere, but right now he was fresh out of ideas, and too hungry to think up any new ones. He'd get some lunch, and maybe by the time he finished it, he would have figured out where to look next.

The first thing he noticed when he opened the door to his hotel room was that a table lamp was on; he was sure he'd turned off the lights that morning.

The second thing he noticed was Zara Sutcliffe, sitting at the desk in the corner, writing something on a tablet. She still had on the yellow suit; the gold coat hung from the back of the chair and her tote bag rested on the floor next to it. "Gage." She stood up quickly. "I hope you don't mind. I tricked my way in here. I found that Doughboy person and convinced him I was your wife. I needed someplace to go, 'cause when I went up to the apartment, my mother was missing and..."

Gage slammed the door behind him and crossed to her in a flash. Gathering her close, he kissed her...and kissed her...and kissed her. Relief and desire warred within him. The anguish and frustration of the past several hours merged into something new and hot and unstoppable...a passion, a need.

He felt her hands raking his hair, sliding beneath his jacket. Pressing her against the desk, he felt her breasts crushed to his chest, her thighs against his. She returned his kisses with the same reckless passion he felt, pulled him closer, closer.

He seized the front of her jacket with both hands and yanked it open; snaps *pop-pop-popped*; she gasped. He filled his hands with her warm breasts as she moaned his name. His heart hammered wildly; his breath, and hers, came in harsh pants.

Reaching behind her to shove the tablet onto the floor, Gage lifted her by the waist and sat her on the edge of the desk, her legs on either side of him. He bent to suck a taut nipple into his mouth. She arched her back, clawed at his hair.

He reached between them and fumbled with her skirt, unsnapping it from the bottom up—one, two, three—just until he could reach inside...*yes*. She was naked beneath the skirt, and hot and wet and ready, and it was so quick but so perfect, so right.

Gage hurriedly unbuttoned his jeans and freed himself. She got that barn-kitten look in her eyes, just for a second, and then she kissed him and took him in her hand, and he thought he was going to detonate right then and there.

Pulling the strip of condoms out of his back pocket, he tore one open and rolled it on in record time.

He shifted to position himself, grabbed her hips to steady her and drove in hard.

She cried out, her body tensing, her fingers digging into his shoulders. He buried his full length within her before it struck him that something was wrong, that she was in pain. And then it registered: he'd felt it, the fragile barrier, even as he broke through it.

No...it can't be.

But she was tight—impossibly, almost painfully tight. And she was grimacing in pain and pushing at him. "Gage, please."

"Easy now, sweetheart." Taking hold of himself, he withdrew gradually; she sucked in her breath. "Easy."

Tears trembled in her eyes; she was shaking all over.

Looking down, he saw blood on himself.

She covered her face with her hands.

"I'll be right back." In the bathroom, he tidied himself and soaked a washcloth with warm water, his mind reeling. She was a virgin and he'd initiated her brutally. He'd hurt her, made her cry. He hated the idea of causing a woman pain, bringing her to tears. Guilt swamped him, yet how could he have known? How could this be? Zara was a divorced woman, for pity's sake.

She was still sitting on the desk, resnapping her jacket with a dazed expression, when he returned to the room. "Come here." He led her by the hand to the bed, where he made her lie down while he stroked the washcloth lightly between her legs. There was a little blood, not much. "How does that feel?"

She shook her head, an arm thrown across her face.

"Good. I didn't think it would hurt that much."

"It wouldn't have, if I'd only known. I would have been

careful, taken my time...." That wasn't true, Gage realized. He wouldn't have made love to her at all if he'd known. You didn't deflower a girl and then fly out of her life; he didn't, anyway. The guilt resurfaced, this time tainted with anger. She'd let him think she was sexually experienced. Now he'd not only hurt her, but taken something precious from her that he'd never meant to take. He felt all the more responsible for her, and protective of her, for having treated her so shabbily, regardless of his intent.

He returned to the bathroom, rinsed out the washcloth and hung it up. She was sitting up and resnapping her skirt when he came back in.

"I tried to tell you," she said, not looking at him.

"That you were a virgin? I don't remember—"

"That I was Emma." She looked up at him now, with those big, hot-fudge eyes. "I tried. You wouldn't believe me."

Gage just stared at her for a moment, and then he sat down numbly on the edge of the bed. They sat there in silence while he thought it all out and came to the remarkable conclusion that this woman, this woman he'd fallen for so hard and fast, this woman he thought he'd gotten to know so incredibly well in such a short time, this woman he'd...he'd...

"Wow." He hadn't even known who she was. A dull throbbing filled up his brain. He rubbed his forehead, wincing when he touched the knot near the hairline.

"What happened to you?" Zara—no, *Emma*—reached out to him, but he rose abruptly and paced away from her.

"I had a little wall-to-wall chat-fest with the maniac who pushed you in front of that subway."

"*What?*"

He heard her rise from the bed, and turned to face her.

He must have looked as unapproachable as he felt, because she stopped in her tracks, her eyes enormous.

"It was right after I left you at your mother's apartment building."

"That's...Zara's building," Emma said quietly. "Our mother's been staying with her, but it's Zara's apartment. I'm—"

"The house in Queens, that's yours?"

"Yes. I moved in a few days ago. Gage, I'm really—"

"Is this how you two get your kicks? Finding gullible guys and impersonating each other—"

"No, Gage."

"Then what the hell is going on here?" he demanded, a lot more heatedly than he'd intended; she flinched and took a step back. "Explain it to me. Can you just explain it to me? And this time make it the truth."

EMMA STUDIED GAGE'S BACK as he gazed out the window, absently fingering the velvet drapes.

"I hate this town," he said quietly. "I never should have come here."

Emma rubbed her arms. The sense of loss she'd felt when they'd said goodbye in front of the Sans Souci was nothing compared to this. At least then, she'd known he cared for her. *I could fall in love with you,* he'd said. *It would be so easy. But I can't stay here.* Now, he'd retreated in shock, as she'd known he would when he found out the truth. He would still fly back to Arkansas tomorrow, but now he'd leave hating her. The dull hurt between her legs, where he'd been inside her so briefly, echoed a heartbreaking ache in her chest.

"Bear with me while I get this straight," he said, turning around and leaning on the windowsill. "You impersonated Zara to sell the ray gun to this MacGowan Byrne."

"Right."

"For two million dollars."

"Right."

He shook his head. "Try as I might, I can't quite wrap my brain wrinkles around the fact that there's a human being alive who's willing to pay that kind of scratch for a movie prop. A long-lost Van Gogh might bring that at auction. But a toy gun in a private transaction? It's just too much money. It doesn't make sense."

"I know, but that's what the guy offered us. Or rather, my mother."

"Right. Your mother. Candy Carmelle."

Emma nodded.

"A movie star without a cent to her name."

"An *ex*-movie *starlet* who lost everything she ever had a long time ago." Including her own children, to the savage vindictiveness of a husband who cared about nothing and no one but himself.

"That's Act One," Gage said. "Act Two opens with you, all decked out like Zara, stopping at her office for the ray gun. Enter the hapless costar, the country cracker who still believes in truth, justice and the American way." He pushed away from the windowsill and took a step toward her; something in his expression made her take a step back. "At first it just seems like he's there for comic relief, but then comes the little Perils of Pauline scene down in the subway, and he gets to stretch, do his action-hero thing—"

"Gage—"

"But it's later that night," he said, stalking toward her as she backed away, "during the scene in the hotel room, when he really shows his range. Suddenly he's the romantic leading man, and he's *amazingly* convincing, 'cause he's a method actor, really feels every part he plays. Unlike the leading lady, who pretty much just puts on a costume and pretends."

She backed into the wall. "Gage, please, I wasn't pretending then."

He flattened his hands on the wall on either side of her head, nailing her with his luminous gaze. "Sweetheart, you were comin' on to me, in case it escaped your notice. Which was fine with me, 'cause I was comin' on to you, too. Only, what I didn't know was that the actress underneath that tarty little costume had never played this particular role before in her life. It was all make-believe."

"Gage, I..." He had a point. She'd flirted with him shamelessly, deliberately set out to seduce him, all the while playing it like Zara.

"I can't help but wonder," he said, "why a lady of your...limited experience...would have led me on like that. Did you really want me to follow through?"

"Yes."

"Why? I mean, you hardly knew me."

"I..." How could she explain it?

"The truth," he growled. "You owe it to me."

Emma swallowed hard. "I'm going to be thirty soon, and...I just...I felt like I was missing out on something because I'd never..."

Swearing under his breath, Gage wheeled around and strode away. "You were using me to get rid of an unwanted hymen." He turned and speared her with a withering look. "Sorry I didn't finish the job. Maybe you can place an ad in the *Village Voice*—'Wanted, one erect penis. Man optional.'"

"Very funny, but it's not quite that simple."

"Have I mentioned how anxious I am to get about a billion miles away from here?"

Emma slammed her hands on the wall. "Gage, listen to me."

"I have. It's been most enlightening." He laughed humorlessly as he dragged both hands through his hair. "You kept up the Zara act because it facilitated your plan to lose your virginity by the big 3-0. I guess it's best I found out about your little masquerade before I did something stupid, like fall..." He closed his eyes, his jaw set. When he opened them, his expression was determinedly remote. "This is for the best. This way, there are no complications when I get on that plane tomorrow. I can wash my hands of you *and* this city in good conscience."

The statement stung, as he'd no doubt intended it to. It really was over between them; Emma couldn't delude herself about that. But she couldn't leave him thinking she was the opportunistic creature he'd convinced himself she was. Taking a few tentative steps toward him, she said softly, "I did care. Or I never could have..." Heat rose from her throat to her face. "I couldn't have..."

He searched her eyes, his expression softening, then reached out and tucked a strand of hair behind her ear. "You didn't care enough," he said, his voice low and rough, "or you would have told me the truth before this."

"I did. I tried. First in Zara's office and then in the cab. You refused to believe me."

He shoved his hands in his pockets and scrutinized the carpet. "I'll give you that. You took a couple of stabs at it— when you weren't puttin' on the Zara Sutcliffe show, and doing an eerily convincing job of it. You got to admit I was getting mixed signals."

"I can understand why you were skeptical," Emma conceded grudgingly. "But I did try and tell you. Twice."

"By last night you'd given up on it, though," he noted soberly. "And that was when it really mattered. Why didn't

you make one last attempt to tell me the truth before we..."
He glanced meaningfully at the chaise longue.

"I didn't want you to hate me. By that time I was..."
Crazy about you. Head over heels. But she couldn't tell him
that now. *No complications,* he'd said. *I can wash my hands of
you.* "I was afraid you'd hate me, and now you do, so I was
right." Indeed, any real affection he might have felt for her
had surely evaporated in light of this afternoon's revela-
tions. If she were to tell him now that she felt something for
him she'd never felt before, and that she thought it might
be love, he would still hate her, and he would still leave;
only she would have humiliated herself. It did not seem
like a brilliant plan.

"I don't hate you," Gage said. "I just..." He turned away,
rubbing his neck.

He just didn't care anymore. Which was worse?

He wandered over toward the desk and picked up the
tablet that he'd swept onto the floor earlier. "What's this?"
he asked, inspecting what she'd written.

"A list. I was working on it when you came. It's just a
way of organizing my thoughts."

Gage sat down at the desk with the tablet in front of him,
retrieved his reading glasses and put them on. Emma came
up behind him and reread her list over his shoulder:

1. Zara agrees to sell Mac the ray gun for $2,000,000.
Why so much? Who is Mac's client?
2. Emma agrees to impersonate Zara and transact the
sale. Gets gun.
3. Gold-eyed man follows Emma into subway,
snatches bag, pushes Emma onto tracks. Just a bum?
Addict? Knows about gun? Police semiresponsive.
4. Emma's house ransacked. Nothing stolen. Gold-
eyed man? Looking for gun? Police unresponsive.

5. Mom missing from Zara's, signs of struggle? Gold-eyed man? Kidnapping? Police semiresponsive.

That was the end of the list.

Gage turned to look at Emma. "You called the cops?"

"As soon as I got here."

"Do they think your mother was kidnapped?"

Emma took a deep breath, dreading that possibility, but knowing she had to deal with it. She'd be useless to her mother if she gave in to hysterics over this. "No, they think she just stepped out to see a movie or do some shopping," she said. "They sound pretty sure of themselves, but they really don't know any more than I do, at this point. They said people are always jumping to the conclusion that loved ones have been kidnapped, but that rarely turns out to be the case, and there's no reason to worry until you get a ransom demand. There was no note left at the scene."

"Are you sure?"

"I looked around and didn't find one."

"I went there looking for you," he said.

"Really?"

"Didn't occur to me to search for a note, though," he admitted. "I'm surprised you had the presence of mind."

"It was my first thought. I took down the remote-access number from the bottom of Zara's answering machine, too, so I can call in and get her messages. If Mom *was* abducted, the kidnappers will probably call there."

"I *am* impressed." Gage was looking at her as if he'd never seen her before.

"I've just read too many mystery novels."

"No, you've just got a naturally deductive mind." He smiled tentatively.

"Thank you," Emma murmured, accepting the compliment as a gesture of cordiality. So. He was going to keep things civilized between them. She supposed that was a good thing. "The last time I called in was an hour ago," she said, checking her watch as she crossed to the phone. "I should check again."

She dialed Zara's number, hoping her mother would answer—*Hi, honey, I was out getting a pedicure*—but no such luck. "They're coming!" shrieked Candy Carmelle's frantic voice on the tape-recorded message. "Don't you see them? You must see them!" Emma held the phone at arm's length, but the scream—a long, full-throated, extravagant howl of pure terror—still resonated in her ears.

Gage's mouth fell open; he heard it from all the way across the room.

"My mom." Emma rolled her eyes.

"Maybe the kidnappers will give her back," he muttered, then winced and quickly apologized.

Beep.

Emma punched in the remote code. There was a message from Zara's hairdresser about a noon appointment she'd missed; that was all. Emma pressed the switch hook and called her own machine to see if MacGowan Byrne had returned her message, or if Zara had called again from Australia; no luck. Emma wished Zara had called. She could be in danger from the gold-eyed man, too; there was no real way of knowing. But not only did Emma not have Zara's number in Australia, she had no idea when her sister planned to return to the States.

Gage picked up the pen and started writing on the tablet.

"What are you doing?" she asked as she came over to him.

"Adding item number six to your list. Gold-eyed man holds knife on Gage—"

"A *knife?*"

"—And demands whereabouts of ray gun. Police vaguely amused."

"What...what did you tell him? The gold-eyed man?"

"That he must be blind, 'cause you've had the gun taped inside your coat all along, and he can come get it anytime he wants, and if I ask him real nice will he please find another train to push you in front of."

Emma snorted. "Har har."

Gage grinned and rubbed the bridge of his nose.

"What?" she demanded.

"Nothin', just...you're kinda cute when you snort." He looked down and started doodling on the edge of the tablet. "Look, maybe things didn't work out too great between us, but I really don't hate you. I know you think I do, but I don't. Just for the record."

"I know."

He nodded as his drawing took the shape of a chaise longue. "Good."

"Sorry to interrupt your artistic endeavor," Emma said as she took the tablet from him, "but I might need this." She tore off the page with the list and stuffed it into the tote bag, next to her jewelry box. Plucking the gold coat off the chair back, she put it on, then hefted the tote.

Gage stood up. "Where are you going?"

"Zara's apartment. I should stay there at least until my mother comes back or someone calls with a ransom demand."

"Maybe they'll call your house in Queens."

"It was Zara's place that Mom disappeared from, so that would be the logical place to wait for a call. Besides, I really don't want to stay at my house, the way it is now. I'll check my machine just in case the call comes there, but I'll stay at Zara's. I'll order in some dinner and spend the night."

"I don't know if that's safe, with everything that's happened. I don't like the idea of you being alone."

"I'll put the chain on the door. I'll be fine." Amazingly, she meant it. A week ago she would have expected herself to crumple in the face of this ongoing crisis, but instead she was rising to it. More and more, she was keeping her head, thinking on her feet, taking action. She'd faced risks and come out unscathed. She'd dealt with strangers without wimping out, and if she found herself on the phone with a kidnapper, she'd deal with him, too. She'd handled things and would continue to handle them, and all without a stitch of underwear.

"I'm coming with you," Gage said.

"Gage—"

"For your protection."

"I don't want your protection."

"Humor me."

"I don't want to humor you."

"If you don't let me come with you, I'll just have to look up your sister's phone number and call you every ten minutes or so to make sure you're okay."

She glared at him. "You know, underneath all that Southern charm, you're really incredibly stubborn and patriarchal and overbearing."

He grinned. "You find me charming?"

"No!"

"You just said so."

"I didn't mean it."

"Did so."

"Did not."

"I'm coming with you."

"Absolutely, positively, unequivocally not!"

8

"Is Chinese food okay with you?" Emma asked, emerging from the kitchen with a portable phone in one hand and a sheet of paper in the other. "I found this take-out menu from a Szechuan place down the street. They deliver."

Gage couldn't tear his gaze away from the tattered poster for *Reptile Bride* taped to one of the doors of Zara Sutcliffe's sleek black entertainment unit. The lurid artwork depicted Candy Carmelle in all her pneumatic splendor, her skin-tight wedding gown artfully torn to reveal a generous expanse of bosom. She was screaming as a reptilian humanoid seized her in his talons. "Huh?"

"Szechuan. Yes or no?"

"Yes." Gage took off his jacket and draped it over the arm of the couch.

She punched a number into the phone. "Hello, Golden Palace? This is a take-out order." She paused. "Sutcliffe. Uh, yeah, go ahead and put it on my account." Covering the phone with her hand, she whispered to Gage, "Serves Zara right for getting me into this... Yes, I'm still here. Okay, let's see." She squinted at the menu. "I'll have a number 17, a number 24 and a 31. Now, when you say hot and spicy, how hot are we talking?" She paused again. "No, I *want* it hot. No, no, no, *extra* hot. Put in twice as much pepper oil as usual. Twice as much. Two times. Write it down."

She waited. Gage grinned.

"Okay, great, and throw in a liter of cola and a couple of pints of hot-and-sour soup. Yes, extra pepper oil in that, too. Thanks. Bye." She rang off.

"Maybe I don't like my Chinese food extra hot," he said.

"Maybe I don't like my burgers well done." She shot him one of those *nyah-nyah* grins that made her look like a mischievously precocious little girl, and it tickled him someplace deep inside his chest, which bugged the hell out of him, because he wanted to be over her completely, and of course he wasn't. *No complications, remember, cowboy?*

"Actually," he said, "I'm partial to spicy food. Somehow I wouldn't have expected you to be, though."

"Virgins have to get their kicks somehow." She tossed the menu and phone onto the couch and grabbed her tote bag. "I'm gonna take a shower. If the food comes before I get out, would you sign for it? I thought we could eat on the terrace since it's so mild tonight."

Gage scratched his chin as he watched her saunter down the hall, open the door to the white bedroom and close it behind her. A minute later he heard a shower turn on.

It was still running twenty minutes later when the doorman buzzed; Gage had to search for the intercom. The guy from Golden Palace was on his way up.

Gage signed for the food and carried it out to the terrace, where he'd already set the little wrought-iron bistro table with plates, chopsticks and glasses. He'd been tempted to raid Zara's well-stocked wine rack, but recalling Emma's lack of tolerance for alcohol, he decided against it.

The terrace, a narrow rectangle enclosed on three sides by brick walls and on the fourth by an ornate railing, looked out onto a secluded little rear courtyard, above which loomed yet more apartment buildings. Dozens of plants hanging in baskets and sprouting from tubs imparted a lushly tropical ambience to the terrace, but left little space for furniture; there was the tiny table with its two chairs, a padded wooden lounge chair with a folded afghan at the foot and barely any room to walk around them. Looking down, Gage saw six identical balconies below him; there were rows of them to the left and right and above him. How, he wondered, did these people keep from going stark raving squirrelly with only fifteen square feet of outdoors to call their own?

He went back inside to hunt for soup bowls in the kitchen cabinets, during which he came across a fat candle in a brass holder. *Why not?* He brought it out to the terrace, set it in the middle of the table and lit it. *Because it's romantic, that's why.* If he was serious about washing his hands of Emma Sutcliffe and this city, he'd kill the atmosphere.

Disgusted with himself, he blew out the candle.

"Why'd you do that?"

Emma stood in the open doorway to the terrace, her skin creamy and golden in the setting sun, her hair twisted on top of her head in a haphazard way that made him want to rip all the pins out and bury his face in it. Worst of all was what she had on: a white T-shirt and a pair of jeans. Button-fly jeans.

"Is something wrong with the candle?" Emma stepped onto the terrace and leaned over the table, her arm brushing his. She smelled damp and sweet, like his mother's magnolia tree after it rained.

"No."

She met his gaze. The low, slanting sun lit her eyes from within; he could see right through them. "Then why did you blow it out?"

He looked down and noticed something he wished he hadn't: she didn't seem to be wearing a bra. Sighing, he said, "I don't know."

Casting him a curious look, she plucked the matches

from his hand and relit the wick. "I like candles." She blew
out the match and sat in the chair Gage pulled out for her.
"In Maine, I had them all over the house. It was the right
kind of house for them, though, a quaint little Victorian. On
winter nights I used to light dozens of them in the bathroom and then get undressed and slide into a nice hot bathtub and read whodunits for hours." She twisted the lid off
a container of hot-and-sour soup and inhaled the pungent
steam that wafted out, her eyes closing in rapturous anticipation. "Mmm. Ready to start sweating?"

"I think I already am." Gage took his seat and opened his
own soup.

He'd thought Zara—or rather, Emma playing Zara—had
been ridiculously attractive. But Emma herself—stripped
of her sister's vampish persona and scrubbed down to her
own true, natural self—was downright mesmerizing. There
was an untouched quality to her, and at the same time, a
peculiar kind of ingenuous wisdom. The combination was
powerfully compelling, and as he worked his way through
the fiery meal, he found himself trying to remember exactly
why he was supposed to be keeping his distance from
her....

*Because she mounted a campaign of deception against you,
that's why. She's no different from the general run of humanity,
lying and cheating to get what she wants. Bottom line: she should
have told you the truth before things got heavy between you, and
she didn't. She didn't care enough about you to be honest when it
mattered. All she cared about was losing her damn virginity.
You're better off without her.*

"Do you think that's possible?" she asked as she snagged
an incendiary prawn with her chopsticks and tucked it between her lips.

"Huh?" Gage's chopsticks kept slipping; he'd never felt
clumsier.

She chewed and swallowed, chasing the scalding mouthful with a swig of soda. "Do you think it's possible that my mother just...stepped out for a while, like the cops said?"

Gage was finding that increasingly unlikely, given that it was almost nightfall and there'd been no word from her. And, of course... "There's the overturned table," he said carefully.

"Maybe she knocked it over by accident."

Obviously, Emma didn't want to accept the likelihood of foul play, not yet. That was okay; there'd be plenty of opportunity for her to freak out when the ransom call came. "It could have been an accident," he said. "Absolutely. She could be out shopping or whatever. No need to start panicking yet."

Emma nodded distractedly and lifted a paper take-out container to peer inside. "There's a little more of the chicken left," she said, tilting it so he could see the torrid tidbits swimming in their bath of pepper oil.

Gage shook his head. The skin was peeling away from the roof of his mouth and he was sweating in places that were physiologically incapable of producing sweat. Also, his butt was griping about the hard little cushionless iron chair. "I know when I'm licked."

"Well," Emma sighed, rising to nest the empty containers together and stuff the paper garbage into the bag the food had come in, "there's one thing we know for sure. The gold-eyed man wants the ray gun. First he stole my bag, probably thinking the gun was in it, and pushed me onto the tracks."

Gage gathered up the plates and bowls and blew out the candle. "Why'd he try and kill you?"

"So I couldn't identify him. If that thing really is worth two million dollars, then stealing it is grand larceny." She headed toward the kitchen with the paper trash; Gage followed with the dishes. "Okay, so he gets home and lo and behold there's no ray gun in the bag."

"So he trashes your house, looking for it."

Emma crammed the refuse into the garbage can, then lifted out the bulging plastic bag and tied it off, her expression troubled. "He knows who I am from my driver's license. He's probably angry at being tricked."

"Yeah," Gage said as he rinsed the dishes, "I'd have to say he wasn't in the best of moods this morning when he got me in that alley."

Emma frowned at the bump on his head. "I'm sorry this has all gotten so out of hand. I'm sorry you've been pulled into it. Really."

He dried his hands on a dish towel, then reached out and stroked her cheek. "Anything for a lady in need."

Emma looked away, obviously discomforted. What could he expect? He *was* running kind of hot and cold.

"I'm gonna go throw this down the incinerator." She carried the garbage bag out of the kitchen; he heard her leave the apartment.

Hands off, cowboy. You're just mucking things up.

Gage poured detergent into the dishwasher and started it, then began to wonder what was keeping Emma. It couldn't take all that long to dispose of a bag of garbage. Suddenly apprehensive, he sprinted to the door and opened it.

Emma was down the hall, by the door to the incinerator. Standing between her and the apartment, his back to Gage, was a familiar-looking steroidal figure in a sleeveless T-shirt and gym shorts—the Neanderthal who'd asked him, this afternoon, why he didn't know Zara Sutcliffe's apartment number if he really was such a good friend of hers.

"And afterwards," the guy was saying, "we can maybe

come back to my place and I'll whip you up one of my special protein shakes."

"I don't think so, Ronald." Emma slid a baleful look toward Gage as he made his silent approach.

"They're good, they're not the soy kind. I make them with egg protein."

"Yum."

"One of those, and you'll be—" he moved closer to Emma and ran a meaty hand down her arm, his gaze fixed on her unencumbered breasts "—superenergized."

"Nice try, pal." Gage closed a hand over Ronald's shoulder; the brute jumped and spun around. "But you'll have to pick some other girl to energize. This one's drinkin' out of my blender."

"You!"

"You two know each other?" Emma asked.

Ronald adopted his silverback-male stance, up to and including the flared nostrils and glaring little eyes. "Mr. Hill and I have met."

"Call me Sam." Gage stuck his hand out.

Ronald studied the hand, his lower jaw thrust out. Any second now he was going to start screeching and swinging from the light fixtures. Finally he grudgingly took the hand and squeezed, igniting a bolt of pain that left Gage's fingers throbbing.

Ronald looked back and forth between them. "So you two are, uh..."

Gage said, "You bet," and Emma said, "Not really," at the same time.

Ronald smiled knowingly. "Seems to be a difference of opinion here. Don't forget, baby," he told Emma, "I'm right there next door any time you need me. You've got my number." With a cocky glance at Gage, he turned and swaggered back to his apartment.

Emma shot Gage a pointed look. "'You bet'?"

He went for a blasé shrug. "Just trying to get that clown off your back."

She smirked and led the way into Zara's apartment. "It's not my back he seemed interested in."

Gage followed her into the kitchen, where she called her home machine, to find no messages—from kidnappers or anyone else—and then whipped open the freezer. "Pay dirt!" She withdrew a half-gallon container of vanilla ice cream. "Want some?"

"Sure."

Emma scooped them each a heaping bowlful. "Would you grab a couple of spoons and the pepper grinder?"

"Pepper grinder? You're kidding."

"Black pepper on vanilla ice cream. Don't knock it till you've tried it."

"I'm not knocking it." He picked up the tall wooden pepper grinder, spun it in the air and caught it, then got a couple of spoons out of the drawer. "I *have* tried it. And I like it, too."

Halfway out of the kitchen with a bowl in each hand, she turned and blinked at him. "Seriously? I never met anyone else who could stand the thought of it."

"Ditto." *Curiouser and curiouser.* She made a detour to the white bedroom, where she layered a zippered, lime green sweatshirt over that white T, worse luck. When they returned to the terrace, they took turns cracking pepper onto their ice cream. Emma sat cross-legged on the lounge chair. Gage, unwilling to put up with those unforgiving little iron chairs any longer, moved the afghan aside and sat next to her.

Night had fallen, making the jungly little terrace seem all the more intimate. Emma's heady, shower-sweet scent enveloped him; he felt her warmth as the air cooled. They ate in silence for a while, absorbed by their own thoughts. The pepper-dusted ice cream reminded Gage of Emma: sweet and spicy, hot and cold. Irresistibly delicious. He considered telling her that, then mentally smacked himself silly.

The altogether different direction of Emma's thoughts became evident when she said, "No one was supposed to know about the sale of the ray gun, right?"

Gage swallowed a mouthful of ice cream. "Right."

She pointed her spoon at him. "Mac told Zara to keep quiet about it—that's why I had to impersonate her. He said if anyone else found out about it, the deal was off."

"But someone else did find out about it," Gage stated. "The gold-eyed man."

"Right." She began vigorously stirring her ice cream into a pepper-flecked mush. "I really doubt Zara told anyone but me about it. The only other person who knew about it was Mac. So that means the gold-eyed man is related somehow to Mac—an employee, friend, relative. Either that or..." She stopped stirring.

Gage shifted so that he was facing her, and met her strangely intent gaze. "I know what you're thinking," he said, "but isn't that guy a legitimate dealer in these things?"

She reclined against the lounge chair's half-raised back and stretched her legs out next to Gage, crossing them at the ankle. "Dealer, yes. Legitimate? I don't know. Zara never did do a proper background check on the guy."

"You expected her to hire a private investigator—"

"You don't need a P.I." She resumed her stirring. "You just need to know where to look. There are professional associations, the city's business-license records, credit bureaus, the local criminal-litigation index, the federal-court index, the IRS—"

"You can get information from the Internal Revenue Service?"

"All I need for a copy of his latest tax return is his name, address and Social Security number."

"How are you supposed to get his Social Security number?"

"By checking New York's vehicle-registration records. Anyone can do that."

Still waters run deep. Gage chuckled. "You really are scary, you know that?"

"Thanks—I think." She lifted the spoon and let the soupy confection *plop-plop-plop* into the bowl, as if testing its consistency.

"I wish I'd known you when I was writing *Open Heart.* I could have used some of that information."

"You mean to say you actually bother *researching* those things?" she asked with an impish smile. "I thought they were just brainless potboilers and you were some kind of hack writer cranking them out."

"Touché."

She regarded him solemnly, her head tilted, her eyes liquid black in the dark. "Why do you belittle what you do? You're a bestselling author. You've got the dream career a million struggling writers—including me—would kill for."

"Oh, it's a lucrative career," he conceded sourly. "And they tell me it's glamorous. But it's not exactly the noblest of professions, you know."

"No, I don't know. I don't see what's so wrong with it."

"You gotta understand." Gage reached over and set his empty bowl on the table. "I grew up havin' it drummed into my head that a man ought to do some good in the world, make a difference. I became a surgeon, and I loved it, and I *did* make a difference. I even saved a few lives."

"You have every right to be proud of that," she said, "but

it doesn't mean that what you do now is any less important."

"I write escapist literature. That's important?"

"It is if the person reading it really needs to escape. Why do you think popular fiction is so...popular? People *need* that mental vacation sometimes. Think about it. Most people really do live lives of quiet desperation. They struggle through their days, trying to deal with the myriad problems that plague all of us—money problems, job problems, school problems, family problems. Life can be rough. The human mind can cope for only so long before it needs—I mean, really *needs*—some kind of break. You give that to them."

Her eyes glittered; her cheeks were flushed. *Don't fall in love with her*, Gage admonished himself. *Don't let it happen.*

"You provide a crucial service to the exhausted young mother," she said, "to the burned-out executive, the despondent teenager. You pick them up and set them down in a different time and place, give them a new and completely imaginary set of problems to worry about. While they're reading your books, their real problems don't exist." She smiled and shrugged. "Think of yourself as a mental-health provider."

"You sound as if you know what you're talking about," he said quietly, remembering her reticence to talk about her childhood.

Her smile dimmed. She looked down at her bowl of runny ice cream.

"Tell me."

"Why?"

He closed a hand over her foot; it felt cold. "Like I said before, it's not morbid curiosity. I care."

Her eloquently arched eyebrow spoke volumes.

"I don't hate you, remember? I hate...what you did. I

hate the fact that you could pretend with me, even after we became…" He shook his head. "There's no point in rehashing that. Look, we both know it's just not gonna happen between us. Even if it weren't for…the other, I live too far away. But that doesn't mean I don't care about you. Hell, I wouldn't be here right now if…damn, I swore again."

She laughed softly, shaking her head. After a moment's silence, she said, "My parents were…unsuited to each other. Extremely unsuited. My mother grew up dirt-poor on Mott Street in Little Italy. She ran away to Hollywood when she was fifteen, changed her name to Candy Carmelle and did her scream-queen thing. My father was a Connecticut investment banker named John Sutcliffe. I'm not sure how they met or why she married him—maybe it was because he epitomized upper-class respectability and she thought that's what she needed at the time. Anyway, it was a big mistake. He was…a monster of respectability. Cold, controlling. And she was, well, Candy Carmelle. What you see is what you get."

Gage massaged her feet as she talked.

"When Zara and I were fifteen months old, she abandoned us and divorced him, and he got custody. At least, that's what he told us. He was a real Nazi with us—we had to live by his rules and follow his regimen or all hell would break loose. Zara caught a lot more flack than I did. I was the good girl—sweet, obedient Emma. Zara was different, more impulsive and daring. My father told her she was a worthless slut, just like her mother, and if she didn't start toeing the line, she'd never amount to anything. He was always punishing her, always putting her down, whittling away at her self-esteem. Of course, he only drove her further away from what he wanted her to be. She became defiant, *tried* to play the bad girl."

"While you," Gage said, "retreated further into the safety of the good-girl role."

"You got it. My father died five years ago. We immediately decided to try and find our mother. It wasn't easy—she didn't leave much of a paper trail. She'd moved around a lot. Usually she was living with some guy, so there wasn't any real estate in her name."

"That was when you learned how to get ahold of folks' Social Security numbers and tax returns, huh?"

"That's right. When I finally tracked her down, it was..." Emma took a deep breath. "Oh, God, we all cried like babies the first time we were together. Turned out she'd never abandoned us at all, of course. She left my father, and when he made it clear he would never give us up—he was rich and powerful, had the best lawyers—she tried to go back with him, but he wouldn't have her. It was revenge, plain and simple. He didn't want us, but he wouldn't think of letting her have us, knowing how important we were to her. I think he might have threatened her if she tried to contact us, but Mom is real vague on that. Sometimes I wonder what she's trying to hide."

Not for the first time, Gage felt thankful for his Norman Rockwell upbringing.

"Of course, that's all in the past." Emma spooned some liquid ice cream into her mouth. "Sometimes I look back, though, and cringe, remembering what it was like in that house, always being on guard, trying so hard to please my father and hoping he wouldn't get mad at me. Mostly I tried to avoid him. I spent my entire adolescence in my room reading mystery novels." She raised her eyes to meet his gaze. "It was my only escape."

"Ah." He smiled. "We come full circle."

"Just as writing *Incision* was *your* escape during med school."

"You're relentless, you know that?"

"I'm right. Being a storyteller is a noble profession." She dipped her index finger in the ice-cream soup; he watched her lick it off, arousal pumping through him. "Admit it."

"I admit it." He watched, enthralled, as she repeated the maneuver, obviously unaware of the effect on him. *Sweet and spicy.*

"You're just humoring me," she accused.

"No I'm not."

She did it again, only this time she slid her finger between her lips and sucked the creamy liquid off. "Ow!" She yanked her foot out of his grasp. "You're hurting me."

"Sorry."

"The pepper adds just the right zing," she observed, dipping in again.

Sighing, Gage plucked a dying leaf from a fleshy rubber tree and fiddled with it as an excuse not to look at her. "I make a double-hellfire chili you might like."

"Mmm, I love hot chili. What kind of meat do you use?"

"Any clean-living critter of good constitution will do, but I'm partial to a two-to-one combination of beef shank and kidney suet."

"Where do you get the heat?" she asked.

"Pretty much anything that'll give you a chemical burn on your tongue if you bite into it. I've got these tiny little chilipiquíns that grow wild around my horse pasture, no bigger than berries, but they're the hottest things I've ever tasted. I like to use them, but any good chili pepper will do—serranos, jalapeños, habaneros."

"I've never used anything but chili powder."

"That's all right, if it's good chili powder, but there's no substitute for the real deal." He tossed the leaf away and moved closer to her on the lounge chair. "First you have to roast 'em and peel 'em, but before you even touch 'em you want to put on some rubber gloves. I use latex surgical gloves."

She smiled in the darkness. "Of course."

He edged closer. "You take a scalpel—or you could use a knife—and slit the chili pod open. And then, if you're a weeny, or you're makin' supper for weenies, you might want to take out some of the seeds and veins, 'cause that's where most of the heat comes from."

"Okay." She was watching him intently.

He took the bowl out of her hands and set it on the table. "Then you put 'em on a hot grill. You gotta keep turning them till they're good and blistered, and then you stick 'em in a bowl of ice water. That slaps 'em awake. Then, if you want 'em really well done—" he brushed the back of his hand down her cheek, over her jaw, along her throat "—you gotta steam 'em in a wet towel. And then those skins get nice and loose. And all you have to do is slip 'em off, real easy." He tugged on the zipper to her sweatshirt, which peeled open slowly.

"What's going on here?" she breathed.

"I think I'm trying to get around to asking you if maybe we shouldn't finish up what we started this afternoon."

The barn kitten. "You mean—"

"It's probably a bad idea." But he kept pulling that zipper down.

"It's definitely a bad idea."

"But that doesn't necessarily mean we shouldn't do it." He opened the sweatshirt and saw her tight little nipples pushing at the cotton of her T-shirt.

"Actually," she said soberly, "it does."

"It doesn't really have to be such a bad idea as long as we both understand that it's just tonight, and that—"

"It's not gonna happen between us," she supplied, using his own words. "You're flying back to Arkansas tomorrow and we'll probably never seen each other again." She wasn't smiling.

He met her gaze steadily. "I don't want to leave things the way we left them this afternoon."

"Half-finished, you mean? I can always take out an ad in the *Village Voice*, remember?"

"I shouldn't have said that. I was a little hot under the collar. But I can't help thinking, you know, that some guy's gonna come along, some guy like that clown Ronald—"

"Ronald is not in the running."

"Well, some guy, and...he's gonna want to finish what I started, and..." He sighed.

"And what?"

"And I think it should be me."

"Because it's your responsibility?"

"Because I'll do it right." He pulled a hairpin from the careless knot on her head; an inky tendril slid loose, and he wrapped it around a finger. "I didn't this afternoon. I didn't know it was your first time, and I was way too rough. I hurt you. I want to make up for that. I'll go slow. I'll be careful. I'll make it as good for you as it can possibly be."

"That's the only reason?" she asked tersely. "Because you'll do it right? That's very noble of you, as usual, but you've done me enough favors al—"

"And because if I don't make love to you right now," he said gruffly, straddling her and closing both hands around her face, "I'm gonna go crazy from wanting you."

He kissed her, an honest, hungry kiss, no holds barred. He exulted in his heart when, after an interminable few seconds, she kissed him back, her arms encircling him, drawing him close.

She kissed a path down his throat as she unbuttoned his shirt, then tore it open and scrubbed her fingers through the hair on his chest. He yanked all the pins out of her hair, luxuriating in its satin heaviness.

He caressed her breasts through her T-shirt; her nipples grew hard as pebbles against his palms. He pulsed with need; it consumed him.

Sitting back on her thighs, he slid the top button of her jeans through the buttonhole...and the next...and the next. He didn't know what he expected—white cotton panties, probably. What he found when he got her completely un-buttoned was much better.

"You're not wearing any underwear," he murmured, ly-ing next to her and slipping a hand beneath the loosened denim.

She turned on her side to face him. "I forgot to pack any."

"You could have worn your sister's." He stroked her slowly, exploring the silken heat of her skin, the wiry hair, the slick, hot, half-hidden mysteries.

"I didn't want to," she said, a little breathlessly, as she fumbled with his belt buckle. His heart pounded; he felt light-headed. "I kind of got used to going without it." She worked at the buttons of his straining fly, her fingers graz-ing him with a maddeningly light touch. He throbbed; his hips quivered with the need to push. When she reached in-side his boxers and closed her hand around him, he moaned helplessly.

He kissed her again, thrusting into her fist, burying his fingers in her damp heat, feeling her swell hotly in response to his caress. She slid her fingers over the drop of fluid on the tip of his rigid cock, and now her grip was wet and tight as she urged him closer...

"Don't stop," he whispered hoarsely.

And closer...

"Don't stop, don't stop."

And...

"Stop." He whipped his hand out of her jeans and closed it over hers, stilling her. "Stop. Stop. Let's go inside."

"Let's stay out here." She sat up and shrugged off her sweatshirt, pulled her T-shirt over her head. "I like it out here."

As she wriggled out of her jeans, Gage looked around at the darkened terrace, at the buildings silhouetted against the sky, black on black with a few dimly lit windows. It was a moonless night, and the dense foliage shielded them from view; no one would see them.

Emma touched his shoulder. He turned around and smiled. She was naked, exquisitely, perfectly, breathtakingly naked, and he wished it was high noon so he could really see her, drink her in, but this would do fine, this was just great, she was...

"Beautiful. You're so beautiful." He smoothed a hand down her arm and felt goose bumps. "But you're cold."

"Just a little."

He unfolded the afghan and draped it over her, then quickly undressed and got underneath it, wrapping his body around her, kissing her eyelids, her cheeks, her lips....

"Better?" he murmured against her throat.

"Yes." She threw her head back, arched her body against his. He cupped her bottom and pulled her against him. "Yes."

They writhed together languidly as they kissed, their breath coming faster, their movements growing ever more insistent, more focused on release. Gage hovered right on the red-hot edge, craving that release like he'd never craved it before; he could take her right now and explode in a matter of seconds, but he'd promised her he'd do this right, and he meant to keep that promise. That meant he had to take it slow, make sure she was ready, that it would be perfect for her.

He slid his hand between her thighs, found the hard little knot of her clitoris, lightly fondling it. She groaned, and he took a stiff nipple between his lips, suckling it as he continued the intimate caress. She tasted so sweet, felt so good in his mouth, so right. He could do this forever.

"Gage..." She raked trembling fingers through his hair, her body going taut, her breath coming in pants.

"Open your legs, sweetheart."

She did. He pushed a finger inside her, both thrilled and daunted by her virginal tightness. She was wonderfully wet, though; that would help.

She took him in her hand and whispered one word: *"Now."*

9

EMMA'S HEART JACKHAMMERED in her chest as Gage felt around for his jeans on the floor of the terrace. She closed her eyes for a moment, willing calm on herself as she heard him rip open the little packet, his breathing as ragged as hers.

He settled between her legs, holding himself stiff armed above her. The afghan slid down, but she didn't feel cold. "Bend your knees, Emma...that's right." He leaned down to kiss her softly, and then he reached between them. "Now raise your hips just a little."

Embracing his waist, she tilted her hips, closed her eyes.

"Look at me," he whispered.

She did. And then she felt a pressure, hard and insistent, where she was so inflamed.

"I don't want to hurt you this time." He pushed in a little, just a nudge, really, but she felt as if she'd been opened wide. "You must be sore from this afternoon, so I want to go slow. Tell me if I hurt you."

She nodded. So far it didn't really hurt—not like it had before, when he'd rammed in so hard and fast. She did still feel raw from this afternoon, but mostly just intensely aroused.

"Is this okay?" he asked shakily, pressing in. He felt incredibly thick, unyieldingly solid, but she stretched to accommodate him.

"It's fine." More than fine; it was astonishing, a gradual

penetration of her body that felt at once so impossible and yet so right. She felt invaded; she felt completed.

Inch by inch he filled her, his entire body rigid with strain. From time to time he paused to let her snug passage accept this assault and relax around him. It worked; he slid deeper and deeper, without causing her pain, until finally, sheathed entirely within her, he sank on top of her and kissed her, a long, achingly passionate kiss.

He braced himself on his arms again and withdrew slowly. "Okay?"

She nodded.

He sank back in with one smooth thrust; she lifted her hips to meet it. He did this again, and again, his expression a strange mixture of concentration and pleasure. She watched him, fascinated by his intensity, by the beauty of his leanly muscled body as it flexed and released. He stroked her from within, grinding his hips against hers when they came together, coaxing her toward culmination.

She banded her legs around him, pulled him down and held him close as they rocked together, not as slow now, nor as gentle, both of them gasping in time with their thrusts, their bodies sweat slicked in spite of the cool night air. He kissed her, and there was something almost desperate about it, and about the way he pounded into her, clutching her too tightly, but she felt the same delirious panic, and it was so achingly sweet that her eyes stung with tears, and she moaned as the end approached....

He broke the kiss. "I can't hold off."

"Don't," she rasped as the tears spilled out. "Come inside me. I want to feel it."

He went still, groaning into the crook of her neck, his only movement a frantic shuddering deep inside her. His pleasure ignited hers; she wept as she came, her body clenching his as if to keep him in there forever, when all they had was tonight.

He held her tight, rubbing his wet face against hers, murmuring something in a strangely raw voice. It was her name, she realized, whispered over and over, like a litany.

EMMA AWOKE to the trilling of a telephone. She was confused even before she opened her eyes, because her phone *rang*, it didn't trill. Once she opened her eyes, she was even more befuddled.

Everything was white. She was naked, and she was in a white room resplendent with morning sunshine, lying on her stomach between white sheets, beneath a white down comforter.

She was in Zara's bed.

As the phone rang again, she turned her head and saw Gage next to her, also lying on his stomach, looking at her, his eyes scorchingly blue amid all that cool whiteness.

He smiled.

She smiled, too.

The phone rang again, and she turned away from him to grope around on the night table—her fingers brushing empty condom packets—until she found the receiver, which she propped against her ear.

"Hello?" she said groggily as she glanced at the clock: 9:42. That meant they'd gotten about four hours of sleep. She felt Gage lower the covers past her bottom, which he fondled affectionately.

A man's silky voice said, "Ah, you *are* there. I just tried your house in Queens, but there was no answer. I don't blame you for not wanting to stay there—the place is a mess."

The voice chuckled softly. Something clicked in Emma's

brain; she heard herself saying, "You should know—you're the one who trashed it."

The fondling abruptly ceased. Gage clambered on top of her and bent his head to the phone; she held the receiver so they could both hear from it.

"Point well taken," the caller conceded, amusement in his voice.

"What did you do with my mother, you bastard?" she demanded. From the corner of her eye, she saw Gage look at her; she couldn't tell whether he was appalled or impressed.

"She's really something, your mother."

Oh, God, he does have her. "Have you hurt her?"

"You've got to admire a woman who manages to stay in that kind of shape at her—"

"What have you done with her, you son of a—"

"She's unharmed," he said indifferently. "For the time being. Interested in keeping her that way?"

"She's my mother. What do *you* think?"

"I think you're going to trade me the ray gun for her."

Emma and Gage exchanged a look that said *of course.*

"That's all you want?" Emma asked. "Just the ray gun? No money?"

"The ray gun *is* money."

"So I gather. Let me talk to my mother, make sure she's okay."

"I'm at a pay phone in Manhattan right now. She's...somewhere else."

"How do I know she's not—" The last word caught in Emma's throat.

"She's alive. You'll just have to take my word for it."

"Right."

"You have no choice," he said. "I've got the upper hand here."

Emma had no argument for that. "How do we make the trade, then?"

"You have the gun?"

"Yes."

"It's going to go down in Central Park—the lake, near the fountain. Meet me at eleven o'clock with the ray gun— you and the cowboy both. Is he there?"

"Howdy, partner," Gage drawled into the phone.

"No heroics, Gomer. This is going to be a clean, simple exchange. You folks give me the ray gun in Central Park at eleven, and I release Candy Carmelle three hours later. I'll let her out near Rockefeller Center at two o'clock—look for her there."

"Why the delay?" Gage asked. "Why can't you just hand her over when we give you the ray gun?"

"'Cause your girlfriend there can't be trusted. Same goes for her sister, and you, too, as far as I'm concerned. No way I'm gonna give you Candy without taking that ray gun home and looking it over real good to make sure it's authentic."

"That's ridiculous," Emma said.

"That's the way it's going to be," the caller said. "And a word of warning. If I catch the faintest whiff of cop while this is going down, if I even casually suspect, for a second, that you've let the police in on our little transaction, I guarantee you I'll make Candy Carmelle scream like she *never* screamed in the movies, and in the end she'll be sleeping with the fishes, catch my drift? Don't call my bluff on this one. I'll do it. Remember the subway?"

Emma didn't bother answering that.

"See you at eleven."

Click.

"That was Mac," Emma said.

Gage rolled off Emma, urging her onto her side and

wrapping his arms around her from behind, so that they were tucked together front to back; then he pulled the covers over them. His body felt so warm, so solid and comforting. "What makes you so sure?"

"Little things. I suspected it, but I wasn't sure until he said he was going to take the ray gun home and look it over to make sure it's authentic. That's something a dealer in these things would say. That was MacGowan Byrne."

"You were smart not to let him know you were on to him. He'd probably waste all of us if he knew we could identify him."

"I'm afraid that's exactly what he intends to do, anyway. Mostly I'm afraid for my mother. Kidnappers don't always let their victims go, even after the ransom is paid. I don't like this business about giving him the ray gun at the park, then getting Mom later. I don't like any of it."

"Neither do I."

She took a deep breath. "Do you think he'll really...follow through with his threat if we call the cops?"

"His threat about your mother?"

Emma nodded. "Do you think he'll...kill her?"

"We have to operate on the assumption that he will. Like he said himself, remember the subway." He kissed her hair. "You okay?"

"Sure."

"I mean, it's your mother."

Emma expelled a shaky breath. "I have to deal with it. It's up to me to make sure she gets out of this safely. I can't afford to fall apart now."

"You've got to be just about the strongest woman I've ever known." Gage tightened his arms around her; she felt the muffled drumbeat of his heart through his softly furred chest.

She shook her head. "I'm faking it. I'm not strong. I'm a dweeb."

A deep chuckle rose from his chest and reverberated through her. "There are some things you can't fake. You may not go through life wearing a Superwoman costume, but you're the kind of person who rises to the occasion, who rallies when the odds are their worst. Your mother is lucky to have you looking after her."

"Yeah?"

"Yeah." He tightened his arms around her even more and said quietly, "I'm gonna miss you, Emma."

She closed her eyes. "What time is your flight?"

"Five-twenty. I almost wish..."

"What?"

Gage sighed and sat up. "Nothing. I'd better get dressed. I've got to be at the lake in Central Park in an hour and a quarter."

"You mean *we've* got to be at the—"

"I mean *I*, sweetheart. You're crazy if you think I'm gonna let you—"

"*Let* me?" She bolted out of bed and turned to face him, fists clenched at her sides. "You really are a patriarchal, arrogant—"

"I'm an old-fashioned guy, Emma. From the Deep South, no less. I'm afraid it's just not in me to let a woman traipse right into the jaws of danger when I can do it for her."

"You were just telling me how strong I am!"

"You are. You're tough and capable and resourceful, and way, *way* too pretty standing there buck nekkid, but I'm still not gonna let you talk me into allowin' you to—"

"*Allowing*? Just how do you intend to stop me?"

"I reckon I'll have to think of something."

"Well, put your thinking cap on...*cowboy*," she said on her way to the bathroom. "I'm going to take my shower and get dressed and catch a cab to Central Park. Because this is *my* mother we're talking about, and it's *my* responsibility to handle this. If you want to come along for the ride, great. I'd appreciate it, in fact. But I have no intention of sitting at home while you're off playing the hero!"

Emma slammed the bathroom door behind her, slapped a shower cap on her head and turned the water on—hot. The sensitive flesh between her legs stung when the shower hit it, reminding her of last night's nonstop lovemaking. The sex manuals with their drawings of copulating couples had familiarized her in advance with the various positions Gage kept coming up with, but nothing could have prepared her for the pure, heart-thumping thrill of it, the frenzied bliss. And then afterward, when they'd just held each other, whispering in the dark, two damp and sated lovers, she'd felt a sense of boneless satisfaction that had awed her.

She'd been overwhelmed, transported. Not just because it was her first time, she knew, but because it was Gage.

And at 5:20 he'd get on a plane for Little Rock and she'd never see him again.

Don't think about it, she admonished herself as she got out of the shower and grabbed a towel. *It's not gonna happen. He's made that clear. So don't torment yourself over it.* She had more important things to worry about, anyway—namely, getting her mother back safely from MacGowan Byrne.

Gage wasn't in the bedroom when she reentered it, but she heard him puttering around in the kitchen; his clothes were gone, so she knew he'd gotten dressed.

In the dressing room she donned a pair of Zara's minuscule silk panties—white this time—reasoning that blue jeans with nothing underneath might chafe her where she didn't particularly care to be chafed this morning. Eschewing yesterday's T-shirt, she hunted among Zara's drawers until she found one chock-full of T-shirts—all silk, Lycra and stretch lace. She pulled on a silk one the color of pewter and turned to the three-way mirror just as Gage walked into the dressing room.

"I put some coffee..." He groaned. "Holy moly, woman, you look like you should be illegal in at least twenty states."

Emma regarded her reflection as Gage came up behind her. The silvery T was pretty and glimmery and hugged her like skin.

"Mmm..." Reaching around her, he cupped her breasts through the slick fabric, thumbing her nipples, which instantly stiffened.

"Gage..."

"Are you very sore this morning?" He smoothed one hand downward until it disappeared beneath her panties, and probed her cautiously.

"A little."

"We overdid it last night. I was greedy, and now you're paying the price." Circling around to face her, he hooked his thumbs in the waistband of the panties and slid them down.

"What are you doing?" She automatically lifted her feet so he could remove the fragile garment and set it aside.

"I'm a doctor, remember?" Sitting back on his heels, he caressed her with a slow, gentle touch that she found as stimulating as it was comforting. He smiled when his fingertips became slippery.

"Gage," she breathed, "this isn't part of some scheme of yours to keep me from going to the—"

"No," he whispered, his breath hot against her as he studied her closely. "I promise it's not that."

He withdrew his hand; she felt a pang of disappointment and wished she hadn't challenged him. But then he lightly gripped her hips, leaned forward and kissed her softly where she was so sore and yet so terribly aroused. He kissed her again and again, light, chastely sweet kisses on her most intimate flesh. It astounded her to be kissed there. Of course she knew people did this, and many times she'd imagined what it would feel like, but she'd never imagined it would be quite like this.

Emma closed her eyes. It was like butterflies landing on her and taking off again, fluttering on hot breezes. She rested her hands on Gage's head, threaded her fingers through his hair, lost in this strange new pleasure.

A rivulet of sensation made her gasp. He'd licked her, a sleek glide, heat against heat. Her fingers tightened on his head. She watched him in the mirror, kneeling before her as he stroked her lightly with his tongue, a soothing caress that grew gradually more inquisitive, more purposeful and rhythmic.

"Gage..."

He closed his lips over her and she moaned. His hands tightened around her trembling hips, steadying her as the dancing heat gathered up inside her. The pleasure was almost unendurable; she ached with it, shivered as it swelled within her.

She heard herself cry out, a low, guttural cry of fulfillment. Closing her eyes, she literally saw stars; the blood roared in her ears. Her climax crested and ebbed and crested again, over and over. Gage pleasured her until she begged him to stop; she was panting and shaking, and her legs wouldn't hold her up anymore.

She sank to her knees; he gathered her in his arms, kissed her endlessly, murmured her name and told her how beautiful she was, how sensual. His hands roamed over her, pulling her against him. She felt his erection through the rough denim of his jeans. "Do you want to...be inside me?" she asked.

He shook his head. "You're too sore."

That was true. "Would you like me to...do what you did to me? I could if you told me how."

He made a kind of despairing groan, but he was smiling. "You can't imagine how much I'd like that. But we don't have time. Central Park, remember?"

He handed her her panties; she stood up to wriggle into them. "How much time do we have?"

"Just enough for a cup of coffee." Rising, he kissed her quickly and left, saying, "I'll go pour it."

Emma threw on her jeans, sneakers and sweatshirt, then went in search of Gage. She found him on the terrace, setting a pot of coffee onto the bistro table next to a plate of buttered toast and a jar of marmalade. There was a jug of orange juice, a bunch of bananas...even that morning's *New York Times*, which had presumably been left outside the door. He'd been busy while she was showering.

She picked up the paper. "Do you really think we'll have time to read this?"

"I won't." He stepped into the living room and slid the glass door shut behind him. "You will."

It took her a second, and then she flung the paper aside and launched herself at the door handle just as she heard the lock click. "Gage!" She yanked at the handle, to no avail. It didn't budge. "Open this door!"

He grinned crookedly from the other side of the glass door. "Enjoy your breakfast."

She slammed a fist on the glass, right over his smug face. "This isn't funny, Gage! Open up!"

"You should be pretty comfortable out there till I get back." He turned and strode to the hall closet, retrieved the gold raincoat and wrapped it into a bundle around the ray gun.

She pounded on the glass. "Come back here! Take me with you! Gage!"

He blew her a kiss and left through the front door.

Emma fumed for a minute, then sat down with a cup of coffee and contemplated the situation. Ever the white knight, Gage had tricked her and gone off by himself to hand over the ray gun to Mac, regardless of the fact that it was her problem, not his, and that he might get hurt, or even...

With a groan of despair, she rose and paced furiously in what little space wasn't consumed by furniture and plants. He should have let her go with him. It was too risky going alone. Mac had wanted them both there; maybe Gage's showing up alone would enrage him.

Could she break the glass with one of the iron chairs? Probably. Should she do it? Not if there were any better alternatives.

If only this terrace faced the street, she could call down to passersby to have the building superintendent come let her out, but there was no one in the little courtyard. She looked down at the half-dozen terraces beneath her and saw no sign of life. Ditto those to the right. But when she peered around the brick wall on the left-hand side, she saw a hint of movement—not on the terrace next door, but in the apartment itself, through the glass door.

That was Ronald Harrington's apartment. She swiftly weighed the disadvantages of enlisting Ronald's help against the advantages of getting out of here, and cupped her hands around her mouth. "Ronald! Ronald, it's Em— Zara Sutcliffe, next door! Ronald!"

The movement continued; she saw the edge of something round and black going up and down, up and down. If that was Ronald, he hadn't heard her.

It took Emma a few minutes to talk herself into her next move. *Do it. Just do it.*

Holding firmly on to the railing, she squeezed her eyes shut and hooked a leg over it. Her stomach seesawed as she thought about how high up she was.

I can't do this. She unhooked the leg and sucked in a few deep breaths.

Dweeb. Just do it. Pretend you're only one story off the ground instead of seven. Emma grabbed the railing again and stepped over it quickly, with both legs, before she could think about what she was doing. She was standing on the outside of the railing now, her sneakered toes balanced on the lip of the terrace, shaking and trying to convince herself she was only one story up.

Carefully she edged toward the brick dividing wall, grabbed it and eased one leg over until that foot made contact with the lip of Ronald's terrace. She clutched his railing and pretty much crab-walked her way over until she was standing on the outside of *his* railing.

She had a clear view inside Ronald's apartment now. He lay flat on his back on a weight bench, red faced and sweaty in purple gym shorts and nothing else, lifting a barbell laden with huge plates up and down, up and down.

Careful, now. It ain't over till it's over. First one leg...*there you go*...and then the other...

"I did it!" Standing on Ronald's terrace now, she turned and leaned over the railing, gulping at this reminder of how high up she was. One false move and... "I must be nuts."

Now to deal with Ronald. Emma rapped on the glass door. Ronald turned, saw her and dropped the barbell onto his throat. His eyes bugged out; his face turned purple. He kicked and strained as he pushed at the iron rod, but with his arms bent back the way they were, he evidently couldn't get the purchase he needed.

"Ronald!" Emma tried the door; it was locked. "Omigod, Ronald!" She hammered frantically on the glass.

Finally, after a heart-stopping eternity that probably lasted only a couple of seconds, he heaved the barbell up with a roar and settled it onto the uprights. Emma leaned her forehead against the glass, mumbling a silent prayer of thanks that she hadn't inadvertently killed this man. She didn't dislike him *that* much.

"Zara!" Ronald slid the door open, grinning broadly. "Wow! This is great! How'd you get out there? Boy, you're full of surprises. Lemme look at you. Come in, come in. You look..." He nodded wanly at her big green sweatshirt, which she knew made her look like a giant version of one of those lime-shaped juice squeezers. "So, to what do I owe the honor?"

Emma shook her head to clear it. "You're not mad at me?"

He blinked at her.

She pointed to the weight bench. "For..."

"That?" He made a *pfft* sound and waved a ham-size hand. "Serves me right for bench-pressing without a spotter. I'm just so glad you finally came over." With a sweep of his arm, he said, "What do you think?"

His living-room floor was covered with mats, the walls with mirrors. It was furnished exclusively with workout machines. "Nice."

His face fell. "Just nice?"

Emma didn't have the time to play this scene out. She had to get to Central Park ASAP. Of course, she had no way to pay for a cab, a complication that hadn't occurred to her till just now; of all the stuff she'd carried around in that quilt bag, the only thing she really needed, it turned out, was cash. "Uh, Ronald, I don't suppose you could lend me a little money. I need carfare."

"Gee, I would, but I have to go to the bank myself. I've got about two bucks in change, maybe, but that won't get you far in a cab."

Thinking fast—she was getting better and better at that—she said, "Can I ask you a big favor, Ronald?"

"Anything."

"I need to borrow your car."

"Absolutely not."

Emma raked her fingers through her hair. "I really need a car, Ronald. I need it desperately."

"Yeah, but *my* car? My new Porsche? Jeez, it hasn't got a hundred miles on it."

Emma wasn't above begging. "Ronald, please. Please."

He shook his head. "I'm sorry, Zara, really, but that car's my baby. Nobody drives it but me." He grabbed a towel off the bench, scrubbed it over his face and slung it around his gargantuan shoulders.

Deciding she wasn't above certain other tactics either, Emma said, "It's so warm in here." She unzipped her sweatshirt and tied it around her waist, exposing the sexy little silk T. Ronald's eyeballs redirected themselves like two breast-seeking missiles. Gathering her hair up, she held it on top of her head and fanned the back of her neck. "Must be because you've been working out," she suggested throatily. "I can almost feel the testosterone."

"Me, too."

"Aren't you hot?"

"Oh, yeah." He hadn't blinked since she took that sweatshirt off.

"I'd take such good care of your car, Ronald. And I'd be so grateful. Extremely grateful. I'd have to figure out some way to thank you. Maybe I could make you dinner, at my place. A nice steak, a bottle of wine..."

"I don't drink," he informed her breasts.

"All right, then. You can make us up a couple of those protein shakes of yours."

He grinned, and now he reminded her more of a dog than a gorilla—a big, sloppy golden retriever. "Yeah?"

"Yeah. And then, after dinner, maybe we can work out together. You can show me your moves and I'll show you mine. How does that sound?"

He nodded excitedly, words apparently failing him.

"Good." She held her hand palm up and took a step toward him, murmuring, "The keys?"

He patted his bare torso and then frowned. "What about Sam?"

Sam...

"Sam Hill," he prompted. "The cowboy."

The entire population of Manhattan had reduced Gage Foster to a one-word stereotype. "He's just a...client. A prospective client. We're not...he's not...he's flying away this afternoon and I'll never see him after that, and *can I just please have the damn keys to the damn car? Please?*"

Ronald backed away, with Emma advancing on him menacingly, and plucked a key ring off a hook by the front door. "It's parked in the basement." He started to hand her the keys, then held them out of her reach just as she went for them. "You *can* drive a standard, can't you?"

"*A standard?*"

"Yeah, of course. It's a—"

"Yes!" She'd just have to figure it out. "Give me those." She snatched the keys out of his hand, flung open the door and slammed it behind her. Halfway down the hall, she stopped, retraced her steps and rang his buzzer.

He opened the door warily.

"Uh...sorry to bother you again, Ronald, but can you tell me how to get to Central Park? Please?"

10

GAGE CHECKED HIS WATCH again—11:19. Mac was late. This had to be the right place, Gage thought, looking around.

He was at one end of an irregular lake surrounded by woods. A round pool had been built here, from the center of which rose a gigantic bronze fountain topped with a winged figure. Water sprayed from the figure's feet, lightly misting the dozen or so people strolling about the brick court surrounding the pool or sitting at the water's edge. Out on the lake, three or four rowboats lazed on the sunsparkled water. There were skyscrapers poking above the treetops, and someone was blasting music from a boom box, but it was the Beatles, so he didn't mind too much. All in all it was an incongruously bucolic scene for midtown Manhattan; too bad they couldn't raze the rest of this island and do this to all of it.

"Mornin', cowboy."

Gage stiffened, expecting to feel a blade at his back. When he didn't, he turned around. MacGowan Byrne wore a gunmetal silk suit over a black shirt. The sun glared off his mirrored sunglasses—a different pair this time. Despite the shades, Gage noted with satisfaction that Mac's left eye was surrounded by an angry blue-black contusion. His bottom lip was split, too. Gage wondered how those ribs felt; he hoped they hurt.

"You're late," Gage said.

"I've been watching you from the woods. Sniffing for cops."

"We didn't call the police."

"Speaking of 'we,'" Mac said, glancing around, "where's your girlfriend?"

"I wouldn't let her come."

"Why not?"

"You need to ask that, after the subway?"

Mac nodded in acknowledgment of the point. "I'm not happy about it, though. This complicates things."

"How so?"

Mac didn't answer that. Indicating the raincoat-wrapped bundle under Gage's arm, he said, "Is that it? Don't tell me she had it under there all along."

"Yeah, we figure you're not as bright as you let on."

The gold eyes narrowed. "We're going over there, into the woods. I'd like some privacy for this transaction."

"What transaction?" Gage challenged. "I'm giving you the ray gun. I can do that right here."

"You could have anything wrapped up in there," Mac said. "I need to see what I'm getting, and I don't think it's such a hot idea, waving a ray gun around in a crowd."

Conceding his point, Gage accompanied him down a path into the woods. About a hundred yards in, Mac led him off the path, into a remote and densely treed section. It was cool and shadowy here, and Gage could just barely make out the faraway strains of "All You Need Is Love" from the boom box by the fountain.

"It's all yours." Gage held out the bundle.

"Put it down there." Mac pointed to a spot on the ground between them.

Gage dropped it.

Mac took off his shades and tucked them inside his jacket. Emma was right; he had wolf's eyes. "Now open it."

"You open it." Gage turned and strode away.

Something whispered past his ear, embedding itself with a *thunk* in the tree next to him. It was a knife, about eight inches long and cast entirely of glimmering stainless steel, with a small hole in the handle end.

Turning, he saw Mac, now several yards away, standing with another one of these things in his right hand, a whole cluster of them in his left.

"Throwing knives." Squatting down, Mac slit open the gold plastic bundle until the ray gun lay exposed. "You did bring it." He grinned at Gage, the kind of grin a cat makes before it pounces. "I guess you're not as bright as *you* let on either, cowboy."

"Why's that?" Gage asked, striving for calm in the face of all those maliciously gleaming blades.

Mac rose and rotated his neck, then his shoulders. "Because now that I've got the ray gun, your usefulness is at an end. From now on, you're just a liability. You've seen me— you can identify me."

"I don't know who you are," Gage lied.

"You could point me out in a lineup. So could that tasty little girlfriend of yours."

"Look, all she wants is her mother back. She won't identify you."

"But she could. You both could. You're loose ends. I hate loose ends."

"Look, fella…"

Mac reared back, his whole body coiling, as if he were about to pitch a baseball. Gage threw himself on the ground as the knife rotated slowly overhead, bouncing harmlessly off a tree behind him.

As Mac released another knife, Gage scrambled to his feet, lurching to the side to avoid it as it spun past his right arm. It wobbled after it passed him, burying itself in the ground some distance away. He could turn and run, but his back would make an excellent target. His heart pumped a mile a minute as he racked his brain for some way out of this.

"Those knives are cute," Gage drawled, scanning the immediate area for the biggest tree, one that might provide decent cover. "But your aim could use some work."

"It's not so bad." Mac pointed to Gage's arm. Looking down, Gage saw that the forearm of his corduroy jacket and flannel shirt had been sliced clean open. Blood trickled onto his hand from beneath his shirt cuff, but he didn't feel a thing.

"It's not exactly a mortal wound," Gage said, "and somehow I doubt you're gonna inflict one with those."

"But trying is so much fun." Instantly, Mac had another one in the air. Gage dove for the nearest tree as the knife hissed past. Panting, he leaned against the tree and put pressure on his forearm, which was beginning to sting.

"Anyway, I don't have to kill you right off," Mac said smoothly. "All I have to do is immobilize you, and then I can finish you off up close and personal."

"What about me?" called a woman's voice. "How many of us are you planning to murder before this is over?"

Emma! How'd she get off that terrace? Gage stepped out from behind the tree to see Mac—too far away for him to stop—aiming a knife toward a flicker of lime green among a stand of paper birch.

"No! Emma!" Gage raced toward Mac as the knife flew to its target. *"Emma!" Christ, no! No!*

Mac sprinted toward the birch trees. Gage followed after him, but pulled up short when he heard a hiss. Turning, he saw Emma—Emma!—gesturing from the trees behind him.

"Oh, thank God!" He ran to her and gathered her in his arms. "I thought...I thought you were—"

"I hung my sweatshirt on a tree to distract him."

"You *are* scary." He kissed her quickly, then grabbed her hand and ran with her toward the path. "Come on. Let's get out of here before he—"

"Gage!"

Turning to follow Emma's line of sight, he saw Mac stalking toward them, letting loose with one of his knives. Gage threw Emma to the ground, his body shielding hers, the knife just barely missing them.

"Somebody call the police!" Emma yelled from beneath him. Looking up, Gage saw the people she was calling to— a group of multipierced teens strolling along the path through the woods, passing a brown cigarette between them. They paused, then continued their leisurely constitutional.

"No cops!" The voice came from a dark figure just visible in Gage's peripheral vision; all Gage saw clearly was the gun in the man's outstretched hand. He jogged past them toward Mac, growling in Emma's direction, "That's a good way to get your mother killed. I'm FBI. I'll be in touch."

Gage and Emma both turned to watch the man race toward Mac, yelling, "Give it up!" Mac swore rawly when he saw him, grabbed the plastic-wrapped ray gun and fled, about ten yards ahead of his pursuer. The two men disappeared into the woods.

Emma craned her head to look at Gage. "FBI? Where'd *he* come from?"

Gage shrugged and helped her to her feet. "They do handle kidnappings."

She dusted off her jeans, picked dried leaves off her shiny little T-shirt. "Yeah, but how would he have found out about...?" The color leached from her face. "What if Mac decides we called the police, after all? He might—he might..."

Gage took her in his arms, cradling her head against his chest. "Your mom's gonna be fine, sweetheart. That guy'll probably catch Mac, and all our troubles will be over."

"My troubles," she mumbled, then added, "But you've made them yours." She looked up at him with her glimmery brown eyes. "Most people wouldn't have wanted to get involved in a mess like this. You've been great."

"Yeah, well, have I thanked you yet for that sweatshirt stunt? You may have saved my life." He tilted her chin up and lowered his head.

"Gage!" Emma took his hand in both of hers and gaped at it; it was covered with blood. "He got you!"

"It's not that bad."

"Look how it's bleeding!" She took off his jacket and rolled his shirtsleeve up, exposing a laceration about three inches long.

"The bleeding has almost stopped," he noted, "and it's not all that deep."

"Deep enough. I think you need stitches."

"Thank you for that assessment, Dr. Sutcliffe, but if I may offer a second opinion, I think all it needs is a nice clean hanky—" which he produced from his back pocket and handed to her "—and about sixty cc's of Dr. Daniels's Throwing Knife Tonic, administered orally, and I'll be good as—"

"You need stitches," she repeated as she tied the handkerchief around his forearm. "Look—the blood's soaking right through."

"We'll compromise on butterfly bandages." He put his jacket back on and took her hand, guiding her toward the path. "We can stop at a drugstore as soon as we get out of this park. And in the meantime you can entertain me by relating exactly how you managed to show up here just in the nick of time."

"Nothing much to tell. I got to the lake and looked around and saw the two of you heading into the woods. I followed you, but it took me a few minutes to find you after you left the path. All I can figure is that FBI guy must have followed *me*."

"Whoa, sweetheart. You're skippin' the best part. Start with how you pulled off an escape from a locked terrace seven floors up and made it to Central Park in less than half an hour."

She sighed pensively. "It's kind of a long story."

"I don't mind."

"It ends with me wrecking a car."

His grip tightened on her hand. "You were in an accident?"

"More like a whole lot of little accidents. I thought I could fake it on a standard, but—"

"Emma, Emma, Emma."

"I made it all the way to the park before it started smoking, but by that time it had been bashed in on all four sides. I'm sure it's been towed by now."

"I hesitate to ask," Gage said, "but whose car was this that took you mere minutes to demolish?"

"Ronald's."

Gage smiled. "Ah."

"It's a...*was* a Porsche."

Gage winced. "Yikes. I'm surprised he lent it to you."

"It took some convincing."

"What kind of convincing?"

"You don't want to know."

After some thought, Gage decided, "No, I guess I probably don't."

EMMA LEANED on the railing overlooking Rockefeller Center's spectacular sunken plaza, staring glumly as the last of the lunchtime crowd paid their checks and walked away from their umbrella-shaded tables. The sun glinted off the gilded statue of Prometheus on the Fifth Avenue side, and a palisade of international flags fluttered in the breeze. It was a crisp and perfect spring day; the plaza and the sidewalk above it were swarming with people, but none of them was Candy Carmelle.

"She's not coming," Emma said quietly.

"She might still—"

"Mac said she'd be here at two."

Gage leaned back on the railing and checked his watch again. She didn't check hers. It had to be close to three-thirty by now, which was when they'd agreed they would call it quits.

Emma chewed on her lip. "Maybe the FBI guy captured Mac and he told him where he was keeping Mom, and she's been released. Maybe she doesn't even know she's supposed to meet us here. Or maybe...maybe she has to, like, file a report or something."

"That could be it," Gage said after a heavy pause.

Why did he have to be so *understanding* all the time? He was really getting on her nerves. She leaned her elbows on the railing and dropped her head in her hands. "He probably killed her." Before the park, there'd been hope, and she hadn't had to face that possibility, but now...

"No." He wrapped his arms around her from behind. "Stop it. Don't talk that way. Your mother's fine."

"My mother," Emma countered shakily, "is tied up somewhere, maybe gagged, too. She's probably terrified."

"Emma—"

"That's if she's lucky." She shook him off and turned around. "If she's not, she's dead. He said he'd make her scream first."

"He just said that to scare you."

"It worked!" Pedestrians all along 51st Street turned to stare at Emma, but she was beyond caring. "I'm terrified. Wouldn't you be, if it was your mother?"

"Yes." He closed his hands over her upper arms. "Absolutely. But you have to try and keep your cool, Emma. You've done great so far. Don't fall apart now."

"I know." She slumped against him. "I hate this."

"I know, sweetie." He stroked her hair, kissed her head.

"I'm scared."

"I know."

"Let's get out of here. She's not coming. You have a plane to catch, and I—I..." She rubbed her forehead with a quaking hand. *Keep your cool.*

"I can't leave you like this."

"I need to get away from here. I'm going to go back to Zara's place. That FBI guy said he'd be in touch—"

"Emma. Did you hear what I said? I—I can't get on that plane. Not with you so upset."

"I'm fine." She backed away from him, not wanting his arms around her, although she wasn't sure why. "No, that's not true, I'm not fine, but that just means I'm normal, because when a person's mother is being held hostage, they shouldn't be *fine*. They should definitely not be *fine*." She sounded like Rainman; she should really get a grip.

"Emma." He reached for her.

She shook him off. "Please. Don't. I just...you have a plane to catch. Go catch your plane."

"I don't want to."

"Bullshit! It's all you've wanted for the past two days! It's all you've been talking about! So go do it. You probably have just enough time to get to the Plaza and pack your bag before the flight."

He grabbed her shoulders and compelled her with his gaze to look at him. "There's something I've been wanting to tell you. I don't know how to say this. It's probably the wrong time and the wrong place, but...I've been thinking maybe I should just try and forget...what you did."

"What I did?"

"Lying to me. Pretending to be Zara. I should just deal with it. It doesn't matter why you did it—"

"What are you saying? You're ready to forgive me? *Me?*" He couldn't be serious.

"It doesn't matter why. I hold everybody to my own set of standards, and that's probably a bad idea. No, it's definitely a bad idea. I just wanted you to know that it's okay. Whatever your reasons were..."

"Well, I don't forgive you," she said flatly.

He just stared at her.

"I tried twice to tell you the truth," she stated. "I *don't* forgive you for refusing to believe me and then, when you finally got hit over the head with the truth, lumping me together with the rest of the worthless, scheming, lying human race and writing me off."

"I didn't. I cared about you."

"Maybe you cared about me, but I was always a flawed creature. Not a noble, upright specimen like Gage Foster. You think you're so perfect, but you're really very judgmental. I didn't quite measure up, but you made allowances for me. And now, in your beneficence, your godly, arrogant, know-it-all superiority, you're willing to *forgive me!* Well, thank you very much, Dr. Foster, but I've had a really rough day, and I'm afraid I'm not in the mood to be forgiven right now. *Or* to forgive. *Taxi!*"

"No! Emma!" He grabbed her arm as she leapt for the curb, arm upraised, but she yanked herself out of his grasp.

"Let me go!"

"You're upset about your mother. You're not being rational."

"I know." She was going to cry again; she felt it welling up and didn't want him to witness her tears a third time. "But I can't help it. I'm sorry. Let me go." The cab pulled over. She opened the door.

"Oh, Emma, please. Please. Not like this. We can't part like—"

"What are we supposed to do, Gage?" she asked in a tremulous voice as she stood in the open door to the cab. "Say goodbye with a civilized little kiss and a poignant remark about it being better to have loved and lost—" Her throat closed up; the tears came despite her determination to keep them at bay.

He closed his eyes; she saw his throat working.

"Because," she managed to say in a choked voice, "and you'll get a kick out of this, the whole reason I didn't tell you who I really was, after we got...intimate, was because—" she swallowed hard "—because I'd fallen in love with you. I know that sounds crazy. We didn't know each other that long. I could hardly believe it myself."

She slid into the back seat and closed the door; he leaned down and looked at her through the window. "Emma..."

"The thing is, I've never been that kind of person, impulsive and so forth, but I did. I fell in love with you. And after I realized it, I just couldn't try again to tell you who I really was. I didn't want you to know I'd been lying to you. I just didn't want to see the contempt in your eyes. You thought I didn't tell you because I didn't care enough. The truth was that I cared too much. Way too much. Way more than you cared."

"I cared a lot," he said gruffly. "I still do."

"But you didn't care enough," she said softly—the same words he'd spoken to her just yesterday afternoon.

"I..."

"'No complications,' remember?" She wiped her face,

calm now—horribly calm. "You can get on that plane and wash your hands of me *and* this city."

He looked stricken. She stroked his coarse cheek. "There's no good way to end this. This way is as good as any other."

He squeezed his eyes shut, then grabbed her around the neck and kissed her, too hard. She broke the kiss and told the driver, "I'm going to East 86th."

"Here." Gage took out his wallet and handed her some bills. "Take this."

"I don't want your money!"

"How are you fixin' to pay for this cab?"

The driver turned and stared at her.

Emma hadn't thought of that. She plucked a five out of Gage's hand with a sheepish, "Thank you."

"That'll do." The driver flipped the meter up and put the cab in gear.

As it peeled away from the curb, Gage slammed a fist on the trunk.

11

EMMA HEARD THE PHONE RING inside Zara's apartment as she unlocked the top lock. *Maybe it's Mom. Maybe it's Zara. Maybe it's the FBI guy.* While she was jiggling the key in the sticky bottom lock, it rang again. *Maybe it's Gage.*

She raced to the kitchen and picked up the portable on the third ring. "Hello?"

"I trust you spent a pleasant afternoon at Rockefeller—"

"Mac!" Emma sank to the floor, trembling. "Where's my mother? Why wasn't she there? What did you—"

"What did you call me?" he asked softly.

Mac. Emma closed her eyes and hissed every swearword she knew.

After a long, unnerving silence, Mac said, "This isn't good. This isn't good at all."

"Look," Emma said in a desperate rush, "you've got to believe me. The only thing I care about is my mother. I don't care who you are. I promise if my mother is returned to me safely, I'll keep my mouth shut. It's just that right now, I don't know what kind of game you're playing with me. I don't know whether she's alive or dead, and—"

"That's why I called," he said. "To let you know she's alive and healthy and even relatively comfortable. I'm not telling you this to ease your mind. I'm telling you so you don't squawk to the police about how your mother's been kidnapped and murdered. Candy's alive and...remarkably healthy, actually." He cleared his throat. "So don't go dragging the East River yet."

"When should I start dragging it?"

"Never, if you can keep yourself from dialing 911 long enough for me to implement phase two of my Candy Carmelle project."

"Phase two?"

"That's the part where I become a multimillionaire and Candy gets the dream life most women just fantasize about."

"Dream life? What are you talking about?"

"You'll find out—*if* you can manage to keep the cops out of things until phase two has had a chance to come to fruition."

"And if I can't?"

"Candy succumbs to a watery death," he said matter-of-factly.

"You could actually do that? To a woman?"

He snickered. "Such chivalrous distinctions are meaningless to me. I wouldn't hesitate to use lethal force if I felt threatened, and gender is not a factor. Perhaps you felt it was, and that's why you let yourself slip and call me Mac."

"No, I..." What was he saying? Was he threatening to kill her?

"You've made me nervous," he said. "I hate having to be nervous."

"Look." Emma raked a hand through her hair. "I said I wouldn't call the cops, and I won't. All I care about is my mother. So don't do anything—"

He hung up.

Emma sat on the kitchen floor with the receiver humming in her ear until it started bleating that annoying off-the-hook alarm. She disconnected, then just sat there, gazing dully at the checkerboard of black and white marble floor tiles.

Finally she stood up and noticed that the message light was blinking on the answering machine. She pressed Play.

Beep. "Ms. Sutcliffe, we need to talk. I'm sorry I couldn't stop and explain things in the park today, but I'm a lot sorrier I didn't catch the son of a..." The voice, which sounded both weary and harried, breathed a raw curse. "Listen, I've really got to talk to you, and I'll try you again later, but I just wanted to make sure you know I'm on top of this, and you can be assured I'll do everything in my—"

Beep.

I'm on top of this....

No cops, he'd said at the park. *That's a good way to get your mother killed.* That was something both Mac and the FBI guy agreed on.

Where had this mystery fed come from, anyway? There were too many unanswered questions, and too many complications. Emma had given Mac the ray gun, but that wasn't enough. Now he'd cooked up some kind of scheme involving Candy, and who knew when she would see her mother again. At least it seemed as if Candy was safe for the time being. Although Mac was clearly a bit deranged, Emma believed him when he vouched for her mother's well-being, simply because he seemed to be seriously trying to implement this lunatic "phase two."

So, Candy was safe. But what about Emma?

You've made me nervous. I hate being nervous.

Me, too, Emma thought. *And I'm sure as heck nervous right now.*

She locked both locks on the front door, then slipped the chain on. Then, feeling like an idiot, she dragged a straight-backed, wooden kitchen chair over to the door and wedged it under the doorknob for extra protection.

Finally she went to the intercom and buzzed the doorman. "If anyone comes to visit me—anyone at all—don't let him up. Buzz me."

"Will do, Ms. Sutcliffe." It was the big, oily, pencilmustache guy—a surreal hybrid of The Hulk and Gomez Addams.

If the doorbell rang with no warning from the doorman, it meant either someone had slipped past him or Ronald had gotten curious as to the whereabouts of his Porsche. If the bell rang, she would ignore it.

Despite her precautions, Emma knew she was too anxious to sleep tonight. She itched to pick up the phone and dial the police, but Mac's image of a watery death for her mother kept coming back to torment her. The prudent option was to sit tight for the time being and see what unfolded...and hope Mac didn't feel threatened enough by her to "use lethal force."

Here she was, panicking at the prospect of becoming a murder victim, when, if things had gone right, she'd be celebrating the return of her mother. Instead, events were getting more convoluted just when they should be winding up. She needed to get a grip, to think the situation through and figure out what was happening here. She needed to make a list—or rather, to add to the one she'd started yesterday. And she needed to chill out with a little tranquilizing aquatherapy.

Deciding to kill two birds with one stone, she retrieved the list from her tote bag, ran a hot bath spiked with Zara's Midnight Magnolia oil, stripped, pinned her hair up and settled in.

For a long time she tried to study the list, to ponder the chain of events involving the ray gun and Candy and Mac, but her gaze kept gravitating down to the little doodle at the bottom of the page—Gage's drawing of the chaise longue in his hotel room.

He'd sketched it lightly and quickly, but captured it perfectly; its graceful curves looked sensual, almost womanly. It looked like much more than a simple piece of furniture.

The phone rang. She dropped the sheet of paper in the water and quickly snatched it out, but not before the ink blurred, fuzzing not only the words, but the beautiful little drawing—her only real remembrance of Gage.

Dismayed, she crushed it in her fist, leapt from the tub and marched into the bedroom, soaking wet. She picked up the phone. "Yes?"

"Emma?" It was Gage. His voice sounded distant, although he was obviously speaking up. In the background she heard the muffled din of voices, including a P.A. announcement. "Can you hear me? I'm at a pay phone at La Guardia."

"I can hear you, but not well."

"Listen, I had to talk to you again, make sure everything's okay."

"Everything's peachy. Mac called."

There was a heartbeat's pause. "Is your mom..."

"She's okay. He's holding on to her, though. He's got some scheme he calls 'phase two.'"

"I'm sorry, I'm having trouble hearing you. He's got some scheme?"

"Forget it, I don't understand it myself." No point would be served, she decided, by telling him that she'd spilled the beans about knowing Mac's identity.

"Is she okay, do you think—your mom?"

"For the time being, yeah."

A longer pause. "I miss you already, Emma." Despite the bad connection, the soft Dixie rumble of his voice sent a surge of longing coursing through her. This was agonizing.

She'd always heard that a clean break was best when you split up with someone, and now she knew why; the pain would be intense, but then it would be over with, not this ongoing torture.

Emma sat on the bed, not caring that she was getting the comforter wet, opened up the damp wad of paper in her hand and smoothed it out on her bare thigh. The drawing had bled until it looked as if the chaise were floating among bluish clouds.

"Emma? They're boarding my flight."

Emma looked at the clock on the nightstand. It was 5:16.

"You'd better hurry then," she said. "It takes off in four minutes." She started to shiver.

"Emma—"

"I'm cold. I got out of the bathtub when the phone rang and I'm wet and I can't stay here talking to you anymore, Gage. We said our goodbyes."

"No we didn't. We never actually said 'goodbye.'"

She took a deep breath and let it out slowly. "Goodbye, Gage."

In the ensuing silence she heard a woman's muted voice announcing final boarding for the flight to Little Rock. She barely heard his soft "Goodbye, Emma."

She replaced the receiver in its cradle, laid the wet sheet of paper on the night table and drained the tub. Searching through Zara's closet, she came up with a white silk kimono and put that on. It felt slippery and smooth against her bare skin. She decided she could maybe get used to silk if she just gave it half a chance.

Unlocking the sliding glass door, she stepped out onto the terrace, only to discover the remains of the breakfast Gage had prepared for her still sitting on the bistro table. She cleaned it all up and then, on impulse, poured herself a glass of Chablis from a bottle in the fridge and took it to the terrace. Some supper might not be a bad idea, but she didn't feel like cooking anything and didn't have any money for takeout. Also, her stomach felt as if it were being squeezed in a fist—a reaction both to Gage's departure and to Mac's implied threat.

Pulling the sheer curtains across the open doorway to soften the light from the living room, she reclined on the lounge chair and sipped the wine slowly, accustoming herself to its sharp fruitiness and the subtle bloom of warmth that enveloped her.

Night fell. One by one, lights went on in the windows of the buildings across the courtyard. Shapes moved around behind drawn shades—people going about their lives, playing out their various daily dramas.

She thought about the pain of losing Gage and wondered how other people managed to tolerate this kind of anguish. And it was anguish, despite that she'd known Gage for mere days. How much worse must it be to end a long-term relationship? She didn't think she ever wanted to find out.

A harsh buzzing jolted her from her melancholy ruminations—the intercom. Slipping through the curtains into the living room, she pressed the button by the front door. "Yes?"

The doorman's staticky voice said, "It's that guy from Plaza Security Systems. He wants to come up."

"Who?" Panic swept through Emma. *Mac.*

"Mr. Hill," said Gomez. "Can I go ahead and let him—"

"No! Don't let him up!"

"Are you sure?"

"Yes. Absolutely."

After a brief pause, he said, "All right," in an if-you-say-so tone.

Her heart racing, Emma rechecked the locks and the stability of the chair lodged under the doorknob. It was Mac, she was sure. He was just calling himself Mr. Hill so that…

Hill. *Sam* Hill. Gage! It was Gage! Gage was downstairs!

Emma reached for the intercom button, but hesitated. *A clean break. It's hard, but it's the only way. Don't let him draw it out. Don't let him up.*

Marching purposefully to the terrace, she lifted her wineglass to her mouth. By the time she'd drained it, she realized something. *He missed his flight.*

He'd always said nothing would keep him off that flight—nothing. Yet he'd let the plane take off without him. And had come back here. To her. She couldn't believe he'd go to that extreme just to say goodbye again.

And she'd sent him away! *Idiot! Idiot!* She sprinted back to the front door and jammed her thumb on the button. "I'm sorry, I've changed my mind. You can let him up."

"Let him up?"

"Ga— Mr. Hill. You can let him up."

"He's gone, Ms. Sutcliffe."

"Gone?"

"Yeah, he turned around and left when you wouldn't let him up. Gee, if I'd known you were gonna change your mind—"

"Forget it," she said. "I'll be right down."

Emma shoved the chair aside, unlocked the door, grabbed the keys and bolted down the hall. She stabbed the button for the elevator, and when it didn't come quickly enough, she slammed open the door to the stairwell, lifted the skirt of her robe and raced barefoot down seven flights.

Her heart was slamming in her chest by the time she ran out onto the sidewalk. "Gage!" A middle-aged couple gaped at her; the man leered. She pulled the neck of her robe closed and peered up and down 86th Street. It was dark, and she couldn't see much, but the few other pedestrians didn't look anything like Gage.

Dejected and kicking herself, she went back up to the apartment, reset the locks and replaced the chair. *Are you happy now? You've* really *screwed things up.* He'd never want to talk to her again, and why should he?

She sat on the couch, willing herself not to cry for about fifteen minutes, then grabbed the TV remote and numbly flicked through channels for a while. "Who watches this stuff?" Turning it off, she went and sat cross-legged in front of the entertainment unit where Zara had a hidden bookcase filled with hardcovers in shiny, untouched jackets, most of them by authors she represented. A quick perusal revealed the collection to be an eclectic mix of literary fiction, big bestsellers, celebrity bios, New Age self-help books and cookbooks.

Emma pulled a literary novel emblazoned with a gold award sticker off the shelf and read the back-cover copy; it appeared to be a tale of divorce and suicide set in a small, Midwestern university town. A second novel of the same breed had to do with crippling illness and divorce. A third and very long one seemed to be an epic tale of madness, divorce and a whole string of tragic deaths.

She jammed them back in their spots. Emma liked books with happy endings. She wanted the bad guys caught, the space monsters vanquished, the hero and heroine to live happily ever after—not because this reflected reality, but because it didn't.

If she wanted real life, she had her own: the bad guy was still running around loose and the heroine had just blown her last chance with the hero. If there were any space monsters in the vicinity, they'd probably be crawling up the side of the building right about now.

A faint scraping sound made her turn toward the terrace.

She stilled, listening intently. A period of silence was followed by an almost imperceptible *thunk*. The sounds emanated from beyond the fluttering chiffon curtains pulled across the doorway to the terrace.

Her gaze was drawn to the poster for *The Slithering*, which featured the monster du jour wrapping its lascivious tentacles around a dripping-wet Candy Carmelle. The full-color art displayed the creature's each and every grasping sucker in minute detail. Something like that could scale a building like this, easy, Emma thought giddily.

A soft grunt—a very human grunt of effort—sent her scrambling to her feet and sprinting for the front door. Someone was out there. *It's Mac.* She unlocked the door with fumbling haste. *He's out there and he's gonna to kill me and there's no time to call the cops, I have to get out of here—*

Footsteps landed heavily on the terrace; a planter crashed and broke. Turning, she saw a dark shadow through the sheer curtains, a hand yanking them aside....

She pushed the chair away from the door, but it was too late; she heard him behind her, closing in on her....

She grabbed the chair, turned and swung it as hard as she could. It splintered. A man bellowed and dropped to the carpet. "What the Sam Hill..."

Gage? Emma gaped at him, the broken chair clutched in her quivering fists. "I thought...I thought..."

He sat up, rubbing the back of his neck. "That's a hell of a way to say howdy. *Damn*, I swore in front of you again!"

She threw the chair aside and knelt in front of him. "Gage, I'm so sorry, I thought—"

He wrapped his arms around her and threw her down, pressing her into the carpet. "Good for you. I could have been anybody. I could have been Mac." He caressed the silk robe from shoulder to breast. "This is real pretty. I like you in this."

"I thought you *were* Mac."

His eyes darkened to cobalt. "Has he threatened you?"

"More or less. He knows I know who he is."

Gage groaned and lowered his forehead to hers. "Why didn't you tell me?"

"Because I didn't want you to worry."

"Were you afraid I'd do something crazy, like walk away from my flight and come back here and climb up seven balconies to see you?"

"You *what?*"

"I climbed up the balconies. Impressed?"

"Yes!" Emma recalled her abject terror that morning when she'd shimmied from one balcony to the other. "You could have gotten killed. And look—your arm is bleeding again. I told you you needed stitches." She shook her head. "I can't believe you climbed all that way with that arm. Why did you do it?"

"'Cause there's something I forgot to tell you. Don't know how it could have slipped my mind."

"What?"

"I love you."

She just stared at him.

"You're right," he said, "I'm an arrogant ass. First I was too mule-headed to listen to you, and then I went and passed judgment on you like I was Lord God of the Universe. You're smart and sweet and sexy as all get-out, and I don't deserve you, but you're stuck with me, 'cause I went and fell in love with you. Hard."

"Really? Gage, I—"

"Wait a minute, I'm not finished. I thought this all up in the cab on the way here, and I want to make sure I don't forget any of it. What I really want is to take you back to Arkansas with me. I know right now's not a good time, what with all of Mac's shenanigans, and I'm gonna stick by you and make sure no harm comes to you *or* your Mom, but as soon as I can get you on a plane headed south, that's exactly what I mean to do."

"You want to—"

"Shh!" He pressed a finger to her mouth. "You don't like New York. I don't like New York. You need me. I need you. And I think you'll like my place. It's out in the middle of a big old pine forest, and you can smell those trees with every breath. I'll fix you up your own little study, where you can write cozy mysteries. Or better yet, you can share mine. You can keep reminding me what a noble thing it is that I'm writing potboilers—you're good at that."

"Are you asking me to live with you?"

He blinked. "No."

Heat flooded her face. "Oh."

"I'm askin' you to marry me."

Catatonic shock gripped her.

"I told you," he said quietly, "I'm in love with you. I'm not letting you go. And if you're thinking we've only known each other for a couple of days, I've got to tell you it doesn't feel like that to me. I feel like I've known you since the beginning of time. I know you with every cell of my body. I know you inside and out, and up and down and sideways, and I mean to spend the rest of my life getting to know you even better than that. Now, I reckon you're probably still mad at me, but you'll just have to get over it, because—"

She wrapped her arms around him and pulled him down and kissed him, aching with joy, and he kissed her back— like he meant it.

"I have gotten over it," she whispered against his lips.

He smiled. "You have?"

"Want me to prove it?"

"You don't have to...."

But she'd already gotten his shirt unbuttoned almost all the way down.

He grinned. "Okay. Prove it."

If you loved TWICE THE SPICE,
double your pleasure with TWICE BURNED,
Harlequin Intrigue #420, coming in May.
For a taste of the exciting conclusion to
DOUBLE DARE, *turn the page and read on...*

Chapter One

Wolf's eyes, Zara thought, watching the man weave through the crowd at Kennedy Airport's international-arrivals building, his feral, golden brown gaze riveted to her.

It struck her then, where she'd seen those eyes. In that painting of a timber wolf that used to hang in her father's den.

A little shiver scuttled up her spine. Exhaustion, she told herself. The flight from Sydney to New York had been interminable, and she'd yet to refine the art of sleeping on planes. On top of that, the geek in Customs had given her short, tight-fitting fuchsia suit a lingering once-over and made her wait another half hour while he took his time pawing through her luggage and ogling her cleavage.

Now she wanted nothing more than to grab a cab back to her penthouse apartment on East 86th and soak the kinks away in an aromatherapy whirlpool bath. Maybe she'd call her masseuse.

Zara grimaced, remembering her masseuse was a thing of the past, thanks to Tony. Her ex-husband's greed and vindictiveness had left her emotionally and financially drained. She'd lost even the privacy she so desperately craved, because she now lacked the means to install her mother in a place of her own.

With any luck, Mom would be out bowling or something and Zara would have a few rare minutes of solitary peace.

With even more luck, her sister wouldn't have screwed up the transaction Zara had arranged. The transaction that would give her back her privacy.

Wolf Eyes was nearly upon her now, striding with single-minded resolve. He was hard to ignore, towering over everyone else by at least half a head, his dark hair pulled back in a ponytail, those eerie, unsmiling eyes locked on her like heat-seeking missiles.

She sighed. *What now?*

Whatever business he had with her, it could wait till Monday and office hours. She refused to deal with it now, when she was mentally fried and both her Movado watch and her internal clock were set at Sydney time. She rationalized that since she'd already made it to Saturday morning, she could ignore this pushy fellow who was still getting through Friday afternoon.

He was probably some hack author who took exception to receiving a form rejection letter from the Zara Sutcliffe Literary Agency.

She tried to veer away from him, but her progress was hampered by the gigantic, wheeled suitcase she was hauling, with assorted smaller, matching bags dangling from it by straps.

Suddenly he was there, planted directly in her path like some damn sequoia, blocking her escape route. She skidded to a graceless stop in her stiletto heels, nearly landing on her fanny when the heavy suitcase rolled into her, driven by forward momentum.

Rather than reaching out to steady her, as any

gentleman would have done, Wolf Eyes flashed a badge in her face.

"Special Agent Logan Pierce. FBI. I need you to come with me, Miss Sutcliffe."

Zara's jaw dropped and she gaped at him like a beached mackerel. *"What?"*

He reached around her and seized the handle of her suitcase. "No time to explain. The first priority is to get you somewhere safe."

"Safe? What the—"

The fingers of his free hand were suddenly wrapped around her upper arm like a steel band. He swiftly propelled her toward the distant exit.

They were halfway there when the shock wore off and her mind lurched into high gear. She was accompanying a strange man—a very large and intimidating strange man—to God knew where, for God knew what purpose. He didn't even look like an FBI agent. Didn't G-men wear suits and ties? This guy had on jeans and a black windbreaker over a maroon T-shirt.

Zara jerked hard against his unyielding grip, to no avail. He didn't even slow his pace. He towed her ponderous luggage with such apparent ease it might have been a toddler's pull toy.

"Hold on!" she cried. "Wait up a minute."

No response. Those stony wolf's eyes never stopped scanning the noisy crowd, for what hidden perils, she could only imagine.

"Mr. Pierce!" She twisted her arm where his long fingers crushed the silk. "Agent Pierce, please! You're hurting me."

"You're hurting yourself. Take it easy."

"Take it easy? Listen, mister, if you don't let go of me

right now and tell me what this is about, I swear I'll scream my head off.''

He stopped, but he didn't release her. He stared down at her, his expression revealing impatience and more than a little distance. His features were strong, not classically handsome but interesting.

Okay, intriguing. She couldn't help it. Behind those cool amber eyes she detected more stories than one man should have.

She almost laughed at the fanciful notion. Her imagination would be the death of her yet. If she could write worth a damn, she'd be a novelist herself instead of an agent.

She tried to sound assertive. ''I need to see your ID again.''

''No time.'' He was off once more. Zara's spiked heels clicked on the tiled floor as he hauled her along, as if she was just another piece of baggage.

Outside the terminal, the air was balmy, the sky clear azure—a flawless May afternoon. Zara squinted against the dazzling sun, wishing she could get to her sunglasses. Somehow, she doubted Pierce would be willing to stop and let her fish her shades out of the carry-on.

They crossed busy airport roads, darting through traffic. All the while he continued to scrutinize their surroundings.

Suddenly it occurred to her that his loose windbreaker almost certainly concealed a holster. She swallowed back a knot of apprehension. Her voice wobbled as they sprinted across the parking lot. ''You said you had to get me somewhere safe. Safe from what? From who?''

''MacGowan Byrne.''

She lost her precarious footing as that sank in, and

would have ended up sprawled on the pavement if not for Pierce's death grip on her arm.

"Mac Byrne?" she squeaked. "The art dealer?" The man she'd made Emma promise to meet to complete the lucrative sale she'd arranged? The man who was going to solve all her financial problems?

"That's the one." He retrieved a key chain and thumbed a keyless entry button. A car chirped nearby—a small, sleek BMW, black with tinted windows and wide tires. He quickly stowed her luggage in the trunk, then opened the passenger door and shoved her inside. She barely had time to pull in her feet before he slammed the door.

He circled the car and slid behind the wheel, his movements swift and economical, as graceful as the timber wolf she'd likened him to.

And no doubt just as dangerous.

He seemed to completely fill the compact sports car, his big body radiating heat and male vitality. Turning the key, he said, "You should be more careful who you do business with. Mac Byrne tried to kill your sister when she went to meet with him."

"Emma?" she whispered.

Zara was drowning. Air. She needed air. She dug her nails into the leather armrest, her chest heaving with the effort to make her world stop reeling.

"Is she…is she okay?"

Pierce didn't spare Zara a glance. "She's no longer in danger. But he's got your mother. Kidnapped her from your apartment over a week ago."

A sob broke through the fingers she clamped over her mouth.

Dear God, what have I done?

A solid, metallic *snick* made her jump—the sound of

power door locks engaging. She glanced at the spot where
her own lock button should have been, only to spy an
empty hole. Her gaze flew to her companion's impassive
profile as he palmed the steering wheel and backed out of
the parking space.

"A little insurance."

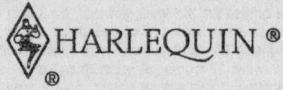

MILLION DOLLAR SWEEPSTAKES
OFFICIAL RULES
NO PURCHASE NECESSARY TO ENTER

1. To enter, follow the directions published. Method of entry may vary. For eligibility, entries must be received no later than March 31, 1998. No liability is assumed for printing errors, lost, late, non-delivered or misdirected entries.

   To determine winners, the sweepstakes numbers assigned to submitted entries will be compared against a list of randomly, preselected prize winning numbers. In the event all prizes are not claimed via the return of prize winning numbers, random drawings will be held from among all other entries received to award unclaimed prizes.

2. Prize winners will be determined no later than June 30, 1998. Selection of winning numbers and random drawings are under the supervision of D. L. Blair, Inc., an independent judging organization whose decisions are final. Limit: one prize to a family or organization. No substitution will be made for any prize, except as offered. Taxes and duties on all prizes are the sole responsibility of winners. Winners will be notified by mail. Odds of winning are determined by the number of eligible entries distributed and received.

3. Sweepstakes open to residents of the U.S. (except Puerto Rico), Canada and Europe who are 18 years of age or older, except employees and immediate family members of Torstar Corp., D. L. Blair, Inc., their affiliates, subsidiaries, and all other agencies, entities, and persons connected with the use, marketing or conduct of this sweepstakes. All applicable laws and regulations apply. Sweepstakes offer void wherever prohibited by law. Any litigation within the province of Quebec respecting the conduct and awarding of a prize in this sweepstakes must be submitted to the Régie des alcools, des courses et des jeux. In order to win a prize, residents of Canada will be required to correctly answer a time-limited arithmetical skill-testing question to be administered by mail.

4. Winners of major prizes (Grand through Fourth) will be obligated to sign and return an Affidavit of Eligibility and Release of Liability within 30 days of notification. In the event of non-compliance within this time period or if a prize is returned as undeliverable, D. L. Blair, Inc. may at its sole discretion, award that prize to an alternate winner. By acceptance of their prize, winners consent to use of their names, photographs or other likeness for purposes of advertising, trade and promotion on behalf of Torstar Corp., its affiliates and subsidiaries, without further compensation unless prohibited by law. Torstar Corp. and D. L. Blair, Inc., their affiliates and subsidiaries are not responsible for errors in printing of sweepstakes and prize winning numbers. In the event a duplication of a prize winning number occurs, a random drawing will be held from among all entries received with that prize winning number to award that prize.

5. This sweepstakes is presented by Torstar Corp., its subsidiaries and affiliates in conjunction with book, merchandise and/or product offerings. The number of prizes to be awarded and their value are as follows: Grand Prize — $1,000,000 (payable at $33,333.33 a year for 30 years); First Prize — $50,000; Second Prize — $10,000; Third Prize — $5,000; 3 Fourth Prizes — $1,000 each; 10 Fifth Prizes — $250 each; 1,000 Sixth Prizes — $10 each. Values of all prizes are in U.S. currency. Prizes in each level will be presented in different creative executions, including various currencies, vehicles, merchandise and travel. Any presentation of a prize level in a currency other than U.S. currency represents an approximate equivalent to the U.S. currency prize for that level, at that time. Prize winners will have the opportunity of selecting any prize offered for that level; however, the actual non U.S. currency equivalent prize if offered and selected, shall be awarded at the exchange rate existing at 3:00 P.M. New York time on March 31, 1998. A travel prize option, if offered and selected by winner, must be completed within 12 months of selection and is subject to: traveling companion(s) completing and returning of a Release of Liability prior to travel; and hotel and flight accommodations availability. For a current list of all prize options offered within prize levels, send a self-addressed, stamped envelope (WA residents need not affix postage) to: MILLION DOLLAR SWEEPSTAKES Prize Options, P.O. Box 4456, Blair, NE 68009-4456, USA.

6. For a list of prize winners (available after July 31, 1998) send a separate, stamped, self-addressed envelope to: MILLION DOLLAR SWEEPSTAKES Winners, P.O. Box 4459, Blair, NE 68009-4459, USA.

It's hot...and it's out of control!

**This spring, Temptation turns up the heat.
Look for these bold, provocative,
*ultra*sexy books!**

Available in April 1997:

OUTRAGEOUS by Lori Foster

He was totally outrageous! One minute, the sexy-as-sin
cop was rescuing Emily Cooper from drunken hoodlums.
Five minutes later, he was tearing his clothes off in front of
a group of voracious women. What kind of man was he...
and why couldn't Emily keep her hands off him? Little did
she know that Judd Sanders really *was* a cop, whose
"cover" left him a little too *uncovered* for his liking.

BLAZE—Red-hot reads—from

LOVE *or* MONEY?
Why not Love *and* Money!
After all, millionaires
need love, too!

How To Marry a
MILLIONAIRE

Suzanne Forster,
Muriel Jensen
and
Judith Arnold

bring you three original stories
about finding that one-in-a million man!

Harlequin also brings you
a million-dollar sweepstakes—enter
for your chance to win a fortune!

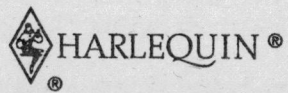 HARLEQUIN ®
®

Look us up on-line at: http://www.romance.net

HTMM

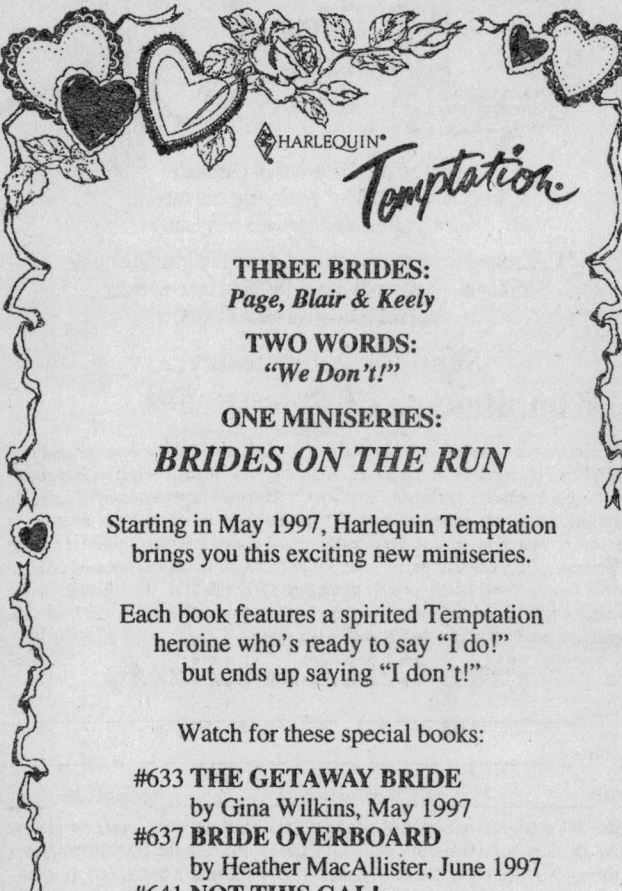

HARLEQUIN® *Temptation*

THREE BRIDES:
Page, Blair & Keely

TWO WORDS:
"We Don't!"

ONE MINISERIES:
BRIDES ON THE RUN

Starting in May 1997, Harlequin Temptation
brings you this exciting new miniseries.

Each book features a spirited Temptation
heroine who's ready to say "I do!"
but ends up saying "I don't!"

Watch for these special books:

#633 THE GETAWAY BRIDE
by Gina Wilkins, May 1997
#637 BRIDE OVERBOARD
by Heather MacAllister, June 1997
#641 NOT THIS GAL!
by Glenda Sanders, July 1997

Available wherever Harlequin books are sold.

Free Gift Offer

As Seen on TV!

With a Free Gift proof-of-purchase
from any Harlequin® book, you can receive
a beautiful cubic zirconia pendant.

This stunning marquise-shaped stone is a genuine cubic
zirconia—accented by an 18" gold tone necklace.
(Approximate retail value $19.95)

Send for yours today...
compliments of HARLEQUIN®

To receive your free gift, a cubic zirconia pendant, send us one original proof-of-purchase, photocopies not accepted, from the back of any Harlequin Romance®, Harlequin Presents®, Harlequin Temptation®, Harlequin Superromance®, Harlequin Intrigue®, Harlequin American Romance®, or Harlequin Historicals® title available in February, March or April at your favorite retail outlet, together with the Free Gift Certificate, plus a check or money order for $1.65 U.S./$2.15 CAN. (do not send cash) to cover postage and handling, payable to Harlequin Free Gift Offer. We will send you the specified gift. Allow 6 to 8 weeks for delivery. Offer good until April 30, 1997, or while quantities last. Offer valid in the U.S. and Canada only.

Free Gift Certificate

Name: _____

Address: _____

City: _____ State/Province: _____ Zip/Postal Code: _____

Mail this certificate, one proof-of-purchase and a check or money order for postage and handling to: HARLEQUIN FREE GIFT OFFER 1997. In the U.S.: 3010 Walden Avenue, P.O. Box 9071, Buffalo NY 14269-9057. In Canada: P.O. Box 604, Fort Erie, Ontario L2Z 5X3.

FREE GIFT OFFER   084-KEZ
ONE PROOF-OF-PURCHASE
To collect your fabulous FREE GIFT, a cubic zirconia pendant, you must include this original proof-of-purchase for each gift with the properly completed Free Gift Certificate.

084-KEZ